T0162151

A HISTORY OF THE WORLD
FOR REBELS AND SOMNAMBULISTS

Jesús del Campo

A HISTORY OF THE WORLD
FOR REBELS AND SOMNAMBULISTS

Translated from Spanish by
Catherine Mansfield

TELEGRAM
London San Francisco Beirut

First published in Spanish by Edhasa in 2007 as
Historia del Mundo para Rebeldes y Sonámbulos
This English translation published in 2008 by Telegram

ISBN: 978-1-84659-049-8

A full CIP record for this book is available from the British Library.
A full CIP record for this book is available from the Library of Congress.

Manufactured in Lebanon

TELEGRAM
26 Westbourne Grove, London W2 5RH
825 Page Street, Suite 203, Berkeley, California 94710
Tabet Building, Mneimneh Street, Hamra, Beirut
www.telegrambooks.com

Seconds Out

On the first day God created light, and he saw that he missed darkness. So he bought himself some black-framed Ray-Ban Wayfarer sunglasses and went out into the street, where he came across humans who, having not yet been officially created, were covering their bodies with paramilitary rags, not realising they were already dressed. He saw them drinking cold beer out of plastic cups and feeling each other's ribs and whispering about the fearfulness of life under the neon signs for Nokia and Kawasaki and General Electric and Holiday Inn. And God went home feeling dejected, wondering what to create next.

On the second day he created music, bought himself a conductor's baton and started practising excitedly with his face to the wall of his study, until, suddenly, he felt a sense of foreboding, stopped humming the *sarabande* he was composing, turned around slowly and saw a group of minstrels gathered together in the centre of the desert, cursing, in a confusion of languages, the unknown force hammering on their temples, as if it would smash them in and abandon them to their destiny of wandering madmen in the middle of that infuriating wilderness.

On the third day God checked his diary and read through his list of creative projects – Audrey Hepburn, the guilt complex, the rings of Saturn, fate, Chartres Cathedral, worker ants – he postponed them all and decided to dedicate the day to creating only lie detectors and hourglasses. But then, on second thoughts, it was all a bit early for that and anyway he didn't like them, so he destroyed them all with a tremendous celestial thunderbolt and that was how, on the fourth day, he created storms. However, something went wrong and one of the hourglasses miraculously survived the destruction and went on to become a cult object amongst the humans, who were now moving about in the fog and the rain, shouting for someone to give them a name to pass the time with. And so, on the fifth day God began to write an ever growing list of names with a stick of chalk on a long jet blackboard, and thousands of people came to consult it; some smiled with relief, others scowled and began to talk of revolution.

On the sixth day God created silence and he saw that it was good, but he hardly had a chance to enjoy it when he noticed that the minstrels, who had reunited again, had split off into two factions of disproportionate sizes; there were a few who were tuning their lutes with silver plectrums, swapping rumours about the roads to paradise and handing out scores amongst the angels; most of them, however, were calling themselves entertainment salesmen and were forming queues outside MTV, surrounded by PR consultants and estate agents from Miami, and God, a little fed up with all this disorder, turned his gaze back to the sea to lose himself in the divine practice of contemplation, and saw a cormorant falling in and out of the waves with its feathers soaked in petroleum.

On the seventh day God made himself a 'Bloody Mary' with two milligrams of Xanax, put his baton away in a display cabinet, rested his head on the *Complete Works of Galileo* and, before closing his eyes, thought what a careless moment of senile distraction it must have been that made him forget to create rest.

Insoluble Lives

The sky was turning a shade of bottle green and Noah knew that the time had come. He finished loading on board his five rubber rings, his fishing rod, his twelve hip flasks of wine from the Euphrates, his bottle of insect repellent and his self-help manuals for combating solitude in the case of floods or hypothermia in the case of shipwrecks, and then, feeling reasonably sure at last of having everything in order, he set sail on the roaring waves.

He soon sailed into sight of the Empire State Building, and saw the president of the United States doing a balancing act as he held on to the lightning conductor while trying not to fall into the copper-coloured water, so close now that it was lapping at the heels of his boots.

'I'm the president,' Noah heard him shout, 'I'm the president and I love Mesopotamia.' And Noah scratched his beard with a gesture that wasn't completely lacking in compassion.

'Just think of Franklin,' he answered from inside the ark.

'The great Franklin liked experiments and believed firmly in the afterlife.' And Noah wouldn't have minded chatting a little longer, but the ark continued on its relentless path, and he had instructions to accept things as they were.

Next he sailed passed the Eiffel Tower and saw Miss France finishing off a striptease on the top, with water around her knees.

'Christian women do it best,' she told him a little anxiously while seductively shaking her minuscule slip of tricolour silk. And Noah shook his head.

'That's an old lie,' he replied. 'I knew the taverns in Baghdad and Damascus and Jerusalem back when the world was still dry, and I bought love many times from the women there, and the slaves from Gaul and Germania were always less intuitive and efficient than the local girls.'

And then he sailed by the Brazilian rainforests and saw a group of lumberjacks who had climbed to the top of the highest trees and were shouting that they worked for multinational corporations but they were against deforestation, and he sailed amongst the icebergs of the Antarctic and read the message of greeting which the displaced Indians had written for him in the middle of the ice with black spray paint and a shaky hand. And he sailed over the flooded Australian outback and saw tattered scraps of the Union Jack covered in grime, and barrels of Fosters beer wrapped in a tangleof rotten seaweed, and surfboards bitten by sharks, and a leaflet about the dangers of sunburn, which caught his eye because it looked like it might be useful. And Noah grabbed a washbowl, tied some string to the handle and hurled it into the water to try and get his hands on the leaflet, but with all the rattling lurches of that unpredictable ark he had no luck with his foolhardy attempt however hard he tried and so, feeling discouraged, he went down to his cabin. He always felt more at home down there, so he took his sandals off, opened his hip flask, sprinkled in some black pepper, took a good swig and was just beginning to abandon himself to that pleasant state of forgetfulness and inhibition which was becoming more necessary to him every day when he suddenly thought to turn towards the raven's cage and discovered it open and empty. And Noah, filled once again with the bitterness of resignation, started reading the Bible while the news on the radio was interrupted by that constant and unintelligible interference which would never allow him to listen to the weather forecast in peace. And Noah fell asleep and had a nightmare in which a naked child threatened him with a round stone and called him a UFO. 'That's a lie, I'm not a UFO!' shouted Noah, bursting with anxiety.

And then his wife appeared with a damp towel wrapped around her head and a cleansing mask of avocado and cucumber covering her face.

'What's all this nonsense about UFOs?' she asked him.

'Sorry,' mumbled Noah, 'I was having a bad dream.'

'I hope you haven't gone and got drunk again,' she said. 'I warned you before we set sail that this whole business would be too much for you, and with all this feeling sorry for yourself you haven't been paying any attention at all to your sons. It's about time you knew that Shem has been accusing Japheth of anti-Semitism ever since he caught him trying on black leather gloves in front of the mirror and theorizing about the survival of the fittest, and Ham has thrown his bottle of shampoo overboard and spends all day long shut up in his cabin wrapped in a cloud of smoke with an unmistakable smell, repeating, with his eyes glazed over, that Bob Marley has all the answers, so I'll leave it up to you to make any sense of that. And when it comes to the animals there's plenty to talk about too; I've been down there for a couple of hours and I won't say anything about the smell because I suppose there's nothing we can do about that, but the problem is that fear of the flood is making them more vulnerable to their own instincts than they were on dry ground. The rattlesnakes are in the cage next to the hamsters, also down to your lack of foresight, I might add, and they're giving the poor little mites some looks that would be enough to frighten anybody. And then there's the Bengal tigers, it seems that the male and the female have taken in upon themselves to start the repopulation and renewal of the earth a bit early, and oh my dear husband, I couldn't help watching them – that's vigour for you, make no mistake! In short, it seems to me that you're missing something, but you don't know what it is.'

And Noah, who always tried to avoid marital discussions as far as possible, was trying to think of some impromptu answer when the door of the cabin was suddenly flung open by a gust of wind, knocking to the floor in a singular spectacular moment a plastic flowerpot containing mandrake seeds, a jar of Earl Grey tea decorated with engravings from the Kama Sutra, and a sepia photograph of Methuselah hunting lions on his 150th birthday. Moved, Noah picked it up to examine it and stroked its silver frame with uncertain fingers, murmuring, 'Truly, it's incredible what a slow and devilish thing time is.'

And then, as he executed the double movement of first getting up to close the door and then bending down to tidy up all the mess, he remembered his wife's reproach.

'Well, yes,' he confessed, 'there's some truth in what you're saying.' And he blushed and scratched the back of his neck and shook his head dejectedly. 'To be honest,' he said, 'I've always wanted to go to Rome and see its palaces and the dome of St Peter's and the Cinecittà Studios; it was a dream of mine that I've had for centuries, ever since I was a lad, and now that we've had the chance it turns out that we haven't passed through that way.'

'Why don't you go and plant vines on Mount Ararat,' she suggested, 'and have a long and happy life?'

'I'd rather sell my memoirs to a literary agent,' he answered, 'but then again when you talk about God nobody believes you.'

But his wife was no longer listening because she'd just seen the empty cage.

'The raven!' she shouted. 'The raven's escaped! Honestly, you're a disaster, the raven was supposed to be a help to us, or had you forgotten about that?'

And Noah looked at his wife. He looked at her with the metallic gesture of a man who has been married for five-hundred-and-seventy-six years without ever allowing himself a word of protest. And then he sighed and shrugged his shoulders.

'Frankly,' he said, 'I'd rather not have any more help from anyone. Salvation is just another form of condemnation, since the desirable thing in a decent world would be not to have to be saved from anything. But then this isn't the right moment to start idealising history. Look, look at those incredible waves, it's beautiful seeing them as furious as they are now, drenching the horizon as if they might swallow that too, and, listen, I don't know what to say, planting vines, well, why not?'

Jonah and the Whalers

They were very surprised to see him appear with his great matted shock of hermit's hair, his face greenish and unshaven, and his eyes so unused to light that the first thing he did was rub them several times, hiding his confusion while he recovered his presence of mind and his balance, and when he found himself more or less steady on his feet in the middle of that great pool of newly spilt whale's blood, he shouted 'Repent!' in a booming voice, making them all step back out of pure amazement.

'Citizens of Nineveh, repent!' he shouted, even louder, as if he knew what he had to say and was ready to say it now that the time had come.

'What's your name?' asked the Norwegian, a burly man who had hair the same colour as his raincoat.

'Jonah,' he replied.

'Not Jonah the Prophet?' asked another sailor, without looking up from watering the deck with his hosepipe.

'Yes,' he replied, 'I was entrusted with the task of

preaching in the streets of Nineveh, and I will keep my promise come hell or high water.' And he'd barely finished saying this when he covered his nose with his hand.

'Honest to God, it didn't smell like this when she was alive,' he said, his face distorted with disgust.

'But in the book it says three days,' a third sailor pointed out. They were all crowded around him, curious and clumsy in their wellington boots.

'Three days, three thousand years, these details aren't distinguished in the mind of He who designs time and has room to hold eternity in His mind,' he answered. 'But how could you understand these things when you only serve to wield your harpoons of death? Repent!'

'But we're a democratic nation,' said a fourth sailor. 'We have an excellent income per capita, central heating for all, powerful feminists and a picturesque royal family. We're a sensible people, who distrust the European Union and read a lot of books.'

And Jonah, who was doing his best to keep up his condemnatory pose, turned around suddenly, climbed up a coil of rope, turned to face leeward, put one hand under his tunic at the height of his inside leg and calmly emptied his bladder all over the gunwale. That was when the fourth sailor felt his curiosity stirred.

'Is it because of our Lutheran beliefs?' he asked. 'Is it because of our relaxed attitude towards sex, or our fondness for alcoholic beverages? If these habits upset you, I ask you to consider the extenuating circumstances of our long and dismal winters, which drive our minds to the very edge of despair and force us to deal with this anxiety in whatever way we can. There aren't many societies better organised than ours in the twenty-first century after Christ.'

'And who the devil is Christ?' replied Jonah in a low voice, frowning as he turned back around to face them, but when he saw their stupefied faces his manner changed.

'No,' he replied, 'it's got nothing to do with those things'. And he looked at the sea, wide and cold and smeared here and there with wandering patches of blood. 'It's because you kill whales.'

'But so do the Russians,' somebody said. 'And the Japanese,' added someone else. And then they all began to speak, very irritably, but in a nice, orderly fashion. 'You'd have to see them to believe it, they're worse than us; the Russians are suffering from a pitiful imperial hangover and have gone and built monstrous hotels where a glass of wine will cost you a working man's wages for a month, and the Japanese eat seaweed, sleep in a sort of niche and play golf in the underground stations. And, fine, the Spanish don't hunt whales but they spend a fortune on the lottery trying to achieve the national dream of living without having to work. And the Danish slander us, calling us savages. And the Argentines spend hours and hours talking about their hypochondria on TV. And the Californians have voted in a governor who measures his triceps in front of a mirror. And there are plenty of other things which we won't go into in detail because we don't want to get you down and so you can go on and prophesy in peace, but you ought to know that in the offices of Amnesty International there are people who spend all day with a map of the world in one hand and a bottle of antidepressants in the other.'

A north-north-westerly wind was blowing hard, and Jonah shivered for the first time from the cold. And then he raised his eyes to the sky, hoping for a sign which he felt at that moment to be well-deserved and urgent, but he found it inscrutable and so had to think fast.

'Which way is it to Nineveh?' he asked.

'That city doesn't exist any more,' said one of the sailors. 'Opposite its ruins, on the other side of the Tigris, you'll find the walls and towers of Mosul in the land of Iraq.'

And Jonah turned back to look at the rough, grey sea and saw that the blood stains had hardly moved at all.

The Great King's Last Day

'There's a big pile of birch wood behind me,' said Beowulf, 'and I have a feeling that it was intended to burn with me inside it and become my final dwelling place.'

'That's men for you,' said the dragon.

'What do you mean?' asked Beowulf. And the dragon looked at him with surprise.

'Well, it's quite obvious,' it answered. 'Men love to surround themselves with the bravery of heroes because they imagine that some of it will rub off on them, but then, once the hero is dead, they feel an absurd, parasitic sensation of transitory invulnerability, as if they could stop being wretched by the mere fact of knowing somebody who wasn't, as if the defeat of another person's courage could redeem them from their own cowardice.'

Beowulf stayed silent for a moment and felt his mind filling with unexpected memories, like a mob of unwelcome guests bursting unannounced into a great hall garlanded with ale and songs. He wanted to shake off the shadows of oars and foam and spears that had once made him feel so naive, and he looked to his left and saw the grey sea. He watched it breaking against the first rocks of the coast, leaping over them and continuing on its path, now a little weaker, until it met the snow and fell upon it, surprised and exhausted, before retreating, in need of more waves to save it from loneliness and suffocation. Then he looked at the dragon, and leaned on the top of his shield.

'So how old are you anyway?' he asked. And his breath formed small, purplish clouds in the pale, crystalline morning air; when the dragon spoke it had no breath.

'Well,' it said, 'I don't really know. There was ice everywhere when I was young, and the sky used to crack every two or three days as if it was badly made, and the men used to tell ridiculous stories about the fire in such a gullible, boasting way that it embarrasses me just to think about it, but too many winters have passed since then and here I am still guarding this damned treasure because, well, you know what the gods are like.'

'You can say that again,' said Beowulf. 'I know only too well. They promise you this and that, they use you at their whim, they squeeze you like a fresh grape and then they spit out the skin and send you off to oblivion for the rest of time.'

'There are minstrels dressed in black polishing their trumpets near the pile of birch wood,' said the dragon, 'and it'll be dark soon; I think it's time for you pick up your sword from the grass.'

September 1066

The young Breton came back and lifted another load of swords and arrows onto his shoulders, ready to carry them on board. In the distance, near the shore, he could hear the horses whinnying nervously; they must have felt clumsy and a little undignified as they attempted the unsteady task of getting onto a boat; they missed their usual habit of marching on solid ground and being admired with their iron-clad horsemen riding on top, and hated having to put themselves, tripping and stumbling, into those hollow wooden devices to cross a sea that was dark and cunning and ravenous for both men and beasts.

He looked around him and saw a group of Norman soldiers who were solemnly supervising the operation.

'They look very calm today,' said his workmate, gasping as he bent down to lift another barrel of wine onto a cart. 'In a few days time they'll have to get down to some serious work and show us what they're made of. That's Huard de Vernon there, and that one is Gautier de Grancourt; take a good look at them, their names will go down in history, unlike yours and mine; there's not room for everyone in the memory of men, time is a castle with restricted access, but the moat around it is crammed with shadows like ours.'

The young Breton looked at them then, and saw them looking back at him, and he realised that just by watching them he could also hear their words.

'Those arrows will soon be raining down on England until it's fertilised with blood,' said one of them.

'And there they'll stay, planted in the ground, and they'll become a forest,' said the other.

And the young Breton turned his gaze towards the North, towards the island that awaited them, and suddenly he imagined a man who was marching towards the South to camp somewhere near the coast with his comrades in arms. And he understood that the Saxon who he had not yet seen and who he might be destined to stake his life against had not always been a warrior, but instead had left behind him thousands of days, days which held many scattered images, some of which were now being revealed to him, to the young Breton who was carrying swords and arrows to load onto a boat. And he saw that the Saxon had once been a little boy who had crawled on all fours amongst cows and geese, and had later reached youth and kissed a young lass on the edge of an oak wood as the sun went down, and had learned how to use an axe forged by another man, who he had spoken with about prices and skills. And this man in turn, in the daily course of his work, had practised the magic of conversation in the Saxon language with many other men who had all gone their separate ways and who were all now talking about the dangers of the coming invasion.

And in that moment the young Breton understood that to imagine just one man was to imagine a kingdom and its marshes and its hills and its nightingales and its storms, and that the Norman army would have to build on top of all that inheritance of mysteries if it fell to them to win and not to die. And he smiled as he realised this, suddenly indifferent to the risks of the battle to come. All the metal and all the enigmas of the world, he thought, are contained in a September's morning.

And his workmate looked at him irritably. 'Get a move on,' he said, 'there's still a lot more weapons to load on board.'

A Lion Heart and Five Dreams

King Richard tiredly put down his hurdy-gurdy, looked out a little incredulously at the grey Austrian forest outside his window and then turned around to take a look at his room and saw that it was still there, just the same as always, with his rusty chain-mail shirt hanging on the clothes rack and his wolfskins strewn over the carpet, and the handful of cherries left forgotten on a wooden plate beside a bottle of Bavarian wine. And then, once he'd made sure that everything was just as it had been the day before, he leaned over the table, rested his head on his arms and fell asleep.

And he dreamed that his mother was riding on a mare outside the wall of a foreign citadel in the middle of the night, underneath a crescent moon, asking, 'Where is my son, fighting for fame?' And a group of monks were telling her, 'We'll show you where he is, if you pay us with a bag of herbs from the garden of Fontevraud, and maybe one or two of those lovely young novices of yours who don't know the world well enough to renounce it.'

'I'll dream it,' replied the queen, and she hugged her pillow with its Flanders lace brocade, and closed her eyes.

And the queen dreamed of a hungry lion lost in a cornfield, pursued by a hunter dressed in a scarlet cloak who was complaining about the risks of bankruptcy while trying to hold a royal crown on his head until, tired of the chase, he fell asleep as well.

And the hunter dreamed of a sultan who was asking, 'Where is this famous Christian called Richard who wants to fight me? Give me my jousting lance and my saffron-coloured gloves!' And his scribe said, 'The Christian has been taken prisoner on the road back to his own kingdom', and 'That's nonsense,' said the sultan, 'that's your dream but Allah knows better,' and then he fell asleep too.

And the sultan dreamed of the castle in Jerusalem lit up by continuous explosions which blocked out the night while a wandering minstrel with a lighted match between his fingers was asking, 'Where is my lord Richard? I fear I've lost my way and I'm running out of light, so I think I should sleep for a bit before I carry on with my questions.'

And the minstrel dreamed of a king with blond hair, his face covered with a mournful carnival mask, who was stroking his hurdy-gurdy as he waited for daybreak opposite a tower where an archer was preparing his crossbow to fire.

A Venetian in Babel

One night Marco Polo decided to stray from the routines of silk and deserts, and without a word he left the caravan and gave himself up to the pleasure of aimless travel until, a few days later, he let himself be drawn in by the uproar coming from the walls of Babel. He rode his Arab horse towards the famous tower, rode up to the first floor surrounded by groups of whispering courtesans and theologians who were looking uncertainly up at the sky, and he met a painter who was sitting in front of a blank canvas with a cup of black coffee in his hand.

'I'm exhausted,' said the painter, 'but I don't dare to fall asleep because I've heard that there's a group of rebels amongst the Babel angels who are planning to fire a round of lightning bolts against the city, and I want to paint that scene at all costs and go down in history.'

Then Marco Polo went up to the second level and saw two angels sitting on the mahogany floor, playing draughts with a pair of submachine guns resting on their laps, swapping stories about women while, about 10 feet away, mute, multicoloured images from the Discovery Channel flickered on TV. With his hardened traveller's instinct Marco Polo knew at once that he had crossed through the pits of time, but this didn't daunt him.

'I've just been talking to the painter,' he told them.

'There are no painters in Babel,' replied one of the angels, with a cracked voice and trembling hands.

'Yes, there are,' Marco Polo insisted. 'I've just seen one sitting on the first floor.'

'Look,' said the angel, 'right now I'm as drunk as a skunk and, since time began there's been no more certain truth than the one dictated by alcohol.'

'But angels don't drink!' Marco Polo protested, shocked.

And the angel gave him a tired smile.

'Well, yes, mate, of course we drink; we knock back bottles of brandy like there's no tomorrow when we're on guard duty and the bad memories of the flood get too much for us. But then I suppose that for someone like you, always so precise when you write about your travels, it must become an obsession to know whether your information is accurate or not, and so with you I'll make an exception and swear by the angelic vice of always telling the truth, and promise you that it is accurate. The fact is that the circles of this tower have become a monument to vertigo and from this height we can all sense the arrival of chaos, and so we've decided to take control of the city and free it from its architects. That's a nice kite you're carrying by the way. It's always funny to see how much the Chinese love their flying gadgets.'

And Marco Polo went up to the third circle and saw a great tree which had been recently felled and had already been turned into kindling, and a hundred prudent virgins were nibbling hungrily on its leaves.

'Is this the tree of knowledge, by any chance?' he asked them.

'No, this is the tree of forgetfulness,' they replied, 'because want to leave this painful biblical phase of sins and punishment behind us.'

And they looked at his hair, surprised to see that it wasn't covered with ash while the sky over Babel was lit up rhythmically by the adverts for Mitsubishi and Jordan Airlines and Deutsche Telekom strapped to the scaffolding of the tower.

And Marco Polo went up to the fourth floor and found half a dozen blacksmiths forging armour for the angels.

'Where are you from?' he asked them. 'You don't have a Babel accent.'

'We've forgotten where we came from because we cut down the tree downstairs,' they answered, 'but things would be different if only we all spoke one language, like that group of economists from the Chicago School who are always monitoring our work, the ones at the other end of the room; it's easy to tell which ones they are, they're always in their shirt sleeves with their ties hanging loose, apparently lost in the study of a map of the tower covered in pencils and compasses and set squares. They say they're only here on a provisional basis to help improve the administration of Babel, but they've brought their own bodyguards.'

And then Marco Polo rode up to the fifth floor and met an angel with his wings cut off, who was sitting in front of a half-written dictionary.

'I was punished,' he said, 'for trying to write the whole thing, before the plans for rebellion, but I come every now and again to take a look at it when I get overwhelmed by nostalgia for the time before the petrol companies came to Babel, when knowledge of the world was still a legitimate goal.'

'Which of the angel armies are you in?' Marco Polo asked him.

'My own,' the angel replied. 'I can't fly now and I'm afraid of the human destiny which is beginning to take us over. Many of my comrades have already tried to escape from here with varying success. One of them emigrated to the Buda Castle and now he spends his days posing completely still for the tourists, who think he's a pretend angel, and on moonless nights he sneaks out and flies euphorically over the Danube and the lights of Pest; another one tried to fly over to St Petersburg hoping he could disguise himself as a statue in the Hermitage and fulfil an old dream of living amongst great works of art, but his wings were scorched to pieces when he crossed through the toxic air in Chernobyl; another one joined up with a flock of cranes but he was shot down over a reservoir in the state of Georgia by a member of the National Rifle Association.'

And Marco Polo rode up to the sixth circle and there

was Eve, sitting on a stool with a glass of Persian cider in one hand and a letter from the Old Man of the Mountain in the other. When she saw the stranger come in she slowly, suggestively crossed her legs and said she'd like to free herself from the hypocrisy of human clothing and become a muse for *Playboy*, but she still felt too young to pose for that foreign insomniac painter on the first floor, and anyway she was fed up with the angels spying on her through the windows every few minutes, nudging each other and trying to be macho, whispering dirty jokes like naughty school boys.

'And all that disorder, for heaven's sake, all that maddening mixture of ascetics and linguists and builders, all living in fear of a simple divine punishment,' she added, 'as if we haven't had enough proof that the history of the world is in the shape of a pendulum.'

The air in the tower was heavy with the smell of a storm, and the Arab horse started whinnying nervously, until finally it refused to go any further, and Marco Polo had to dismount and walk up to the seventh circle, where a sudden gust of wind snatched the kite from his hands and forced his eyes shut. When he opened them again, he found himself facing the endless desert and he saw a scattering of singed bushes and the skeleton of a snake in the middle of the blackened sand, and he heard the beating of wings rumbling like thunder and getting ever closer, and he looked up to see a sky spattered with blood. The kite, lost in the distance, looked like a wounded butterfly.

Horsemen and Conquerors

While the warriors were sacking the city of Kiev, one of them went into a smoke-filled house and rescued a chessboard from the rubble. He tied it to his saddle and then turned back to the welcoming desolation of the steppe. Fierce winds and rain as sharp as lances struck him in the face. And over the years he learned to move the pieces confidently around that battlefield, which, like Khan's armies, had its own laws and disciplines.

His son kept the chessboard as the years passed in the lands of the Empire. And he too carried it on his saddle on the day when the city of Baghdad was taken. He heard the short-lived cries of the defeated, but this was familiar music to the Mongol horsemen, and they no longer cared for it. Once, while camping in the middle of the desert, he played a game under the wintry trembling of the stars against a man who defeated him, while another sat cleaning his bow outside his tent, a few steps away, neither seeing them nor seen by them.

And his son's son also carried the chessboard attached to his saddle, and one day set off with thousands of warriors to cross the seas and conquer the islands of Japan. An enemy wind sank his ship. The men died and the chessboard dropped to the bottom of the voracious waters, and it lies there growing older to this day.

Little More than Love and Death

Romeo ran across the garden, dodging his own shadow, and stopped, gasping for breath, underneath the balcony, while above him, in her room, Juliet untangled her long, reddish hair in front of the mirror, shook her pillow irritably, sprinkled a few drops of orange-blossom water onto a bunch of withered forget-me-nots and contemplated her Keith Richards poster as if thinking about moving it to another wall. When she heard him whisper, 'Come out and see me Juliet', she turned her head.

'Look, young man,' she said, 'I don't know you and I'm surprised to see you here. I'm being kept for a marriage of convenience with an arthritic old man who runs a business in flame-throwers and sails a private boat around islands full of disinherited gods; it's a family thing, and I think you'd better go away.'

'But I'm here in your garden in the name of love!' Romeo groaned. Juliet went back into her room for a moment and came out again carrying a pocket dictionary.

'What was that word again?' she asked.

'I've forgotten it now,' he answered, with his voice at breaking point. 'Some unknown, tyrannical force, moving far faster than my words, has driven me here to seduce you, and oh Juliet, if only I could just see your shoulders!'

And Juliet, unshaken, showed him her shoulders and turned around and dropped her nightdress so he could see her back as well.

'Oh!' he implored her, 'If only I could come up to your balcony and share your telescope with you so I could dream by your side!'

'How do you know I've got a telescope?'

Romeo scratched his head and was grateful to the darkness of the night for hiding his embarrassment.

'Well,' he said, 'in medieval cities all people ever do is talk about their neighbours, and you Capulets are very well known. You come from a family of stargazers. Your father spent years driving a caravan around Arabia, and kept his eyes on the blackness of the skies as he picked weeds from the sand and kept them carefully in a taffeta bag, before trading with the Byzantines and the Venetians and settling in Verona, where he set up his famous apothecary shop which you slip into secretly from time and time to mess around with experiments and try things that you shouldn't try; and your grandfather was declared a heretic and covered in tar in a piazza in Rome for giving names to various stars. And, what's more, he called one Romeo and predicted that it would light up your life.'

'That's not true,' she said, blushing. 'It wasn't a star,

it was a comet that just crosses the night once, and never returns. And you can say what you like about the antidotes, but all I'm looking for is a cure for the poison of youth; that burning torch planted in a field of ice. Look, Romeo, I'll be honest with you. I've got a computer science exam tomorrow, and I hate that damned subject. All I've ever wanted is to be an actress so I can play at being someone else. You don't know how happy it would make me to tread the boards for just one night at the Avignon Festival and recite magical words in front of an invisible audience.'

'You could play at loving your future husband,' he said.

'I will,' she replied. 'They've given me a portrait of him, and I know that he breeds silk worms in his spare time and is looked after by twenty-one multilingual secretaries.'

'Well then,' he begged her, 'if you're going to spend your life acting and pretending, can't you be yourself just for a few seconds?'

'Nobody is ever themselves,' she answered with an infinitely sad, warning smile that passed him by unnoticed. 'That brief fantasy of being oneself died out long ago, when people still went around calling each other brother and sister and talking about the zodiac and living under trees. For heaven's sake, Romeo, it's the strangest thing; the more I talk to you, the younger you seem to me.'

'I want to be your lover,' he said. And his words faltered in the air like insomniac butterflies.

'I want to be your oblivion,' she said. And her words ripped through the blue silence of the night like a dagger plunged into a satin veil.

And then Juliet looked quickly left and right, took off her nightdress and climbed naked down the vines on her balcony until her feet touched the ground of the garden, and she stood on tiptoes in front of Romeo and grabbed him by the hair and searched for his lips and gave him a short, ferocious kiss.

'Now go,' she said in an urgent whisper. 'Go before you bump into some nosey writer on the way back to your house, before the bells of Santa Toscana and Santa Anastasia and San Zeno Maggiore break the night into pieces and the morning makes us fade away, before I start thinking about life and death –'

'What's death?' he asked.

'I don't know, but tonight I saw it written on my computer screen,' she answered. 'I was reading it when you called me, I was drinking from that greenish infusion which tonight tastes so bitter-sweet, and I can feel it making my eyes cloud over, and where are you Romeo, *where are you?*'

The Days That We Have Seen

They could hear the sound of birdsong scattered amongst the great trees of the forest.

'That's a nightingale,' said Jack, lying on the grass, his cheeks damp with dew.

'And that's a blackbird,' said Jane, who also looked tousled as they lay, side by side, half hidden in the middle of the meadow.

'And that's a cuckoo,' said Robert, sitting a few steps away. 'He's probably spreading stories that he heard from us.' And all three of them burst out laughing at once.

'When I see myself lying here as I so love to do, with the sweet Dorset ale coursing through my veins and lifting my spirit,' said Jack, 'I feel as if I wasn't lying on my back on the earth but quite the opposite, resting somewhere high on a balcony and looking down on the grey tides of dawn.'

And Jane smiled sleepily.

'Rumour has it,' she said, 'that our soldiers are bringing back silver spoons from France, and woven tablecloths worthy of a bishop's palace, and our young Prince Edward is a promising soldier who frightens off danger as bravely as he seeks it.'

Robert was quiet for a moment before answering.

'That's all very well,' he said, disdainfully, 'but France is a long way away as far as I'm concerned, and the blades of the weapons can chatter away as long as they like in the only language they know; but please just be quiet for a moment, I pray you, and listen carefully: the cuckoo is singing right now from some part of the wood, and I'd like to discover exactly where it is, on which branch of which tree in this dense English forest around us; from such a narrow hiding place amongst the foliage, it sends such a broad message across the fields.'

And Jane put on a face of pure indifference; she had never liked Robert.

'What do you think, Jack?' she asked. 'You always look so gawky and skinny lying there, as if the grass could swallow you up.'

Jack took some time to reply, lost as he was in his own thoughts.

'I understand,' he finally murmured, 'that the king wants to expand his new order of the Garter, created for the glory of chivalry; and well, how do you like my thigh? It's firm despite its slimness and as worthy of boasting the royal insignia as it is deserving of your praise, Jane.'

And she started to laugh again.

'On my word, what lovely suede breeches you're wearing,' she told him. 'They must earn you such adoration amongst the women of Eastcheap, attentive as they are with you handsome students!'

'Yes, yes, all this talk of foreign victories is all very well,' Robert insisted, 'but it always comes in a much duller language than this rosy dawn, this silent gift of an English summer that crowds around us today like an accomplice in our happiness.'

'I for one don't want to look any further ahead than this moment,' said Jack. 'Right now I'm young and I don't care a bit if these words of ours are lost one day somewhere in the labyrinth of my memory.'

'Jack Falstaff,' said Jane, 'you must be one of the greatest drinkers in all of England, and since yesterday evening you've been the terror of five inns of the parish. You've jumped up on a barrel of anchovies while proclaiming that you were a genteel knight errant in search of a golden age, and you winked at Barry the Miller's wife, and I saw her look right back at you without even blushing, and you danced a jig with a peach balanced on your head as you crossed the bridge, and now, after all these exploits, here you are lying on the grass as if nothing at all had come to pass, not even time.'

'Time doesn't pass,' said Jack in a faraway voice.

'Of course it does,' said Jane. 'It's been three hours already since the bells chimed for midnight, or didn't you hear them?'

'No,' he replied, 'no, I didn't hear them.'

The Waning Moon

The sentinel standing guard on the tower of the Alhambra looked first up to the sky and found it as dark as a mourning veil, scarcely unpicked by a timid, waning half moon, which only appeared to be calm. Then he looked towards the dark North, the hostile North that extended out beyond the confines of the kingdom of Granada, and imagined it populated with Christians who would now have surrendered themselves to sleep, just like the believers. They too would be under the protection of men who, like him, were studying the science of silence.

'The infidels are coming ever further South', he said to his companion without turning his head.

'The jasmine blossoms smell beautiful in the night-time,' he heard him reply.

Saints and Pilgrims

'That's London,' said the knight. 'Look at the red roofs covered in ivy, the pigs wallowing in mud in the yards, and St Olaf's church on the other side of the river, in Southwark. That's where we're going, that's where we'll find our lodgings.'

And his son turned to look behind him without taking any notice of his father.

'Where's the archer?' he asked.

'Well, you know how it is,' said the knight, 'he thought he'd let his hair down a bit before he started on his pilgrimage, and he answered the call of a woman a couple of minutes ago, beside the orchard wall. I have to admit she was pretty; I saw her face for a moment amongst a clump of bilberry bushes. But look here, stop thinking about that and listen to me. Look at London – it's a wonderful place. Look at the Tower and the Docklands skyscrapers and the British Airways London Eye, so tall and so magnificent that when you go right to the top on a clear day you can see as far as Windsor!'

'Yes, father,' said the young man, 'that's all very well, but the fact is I'm used to courtly love and not to paying for it. I hope the archer takes off his silver St Christopher while he does ... well, you know.'

And the knight sighed deeply. 'Look, lad,' he said, 'I've travelled all over the world. I've hunted bears in the forests of Lithuania with the Teutonic Knights, and the skins of those beasts hang today in the great hall of the castle of Marienburg; I've ridden through the south of Spain while the plague was wiping out the Castilian warriors, who each morning mopped their bread in bull's blood before charging against the walls of Algeciras, a fortress enchanted by the idols of the infidels; I've explored the rocky plains of Turkey, again fighting for the cross, and I was once taken prisoner there in an enemy ambush, and I tried their hash cakes with some curiosity, and I won't deny, with a certain special pleasure which I've stayed faithful to across the years; I even managed to learn a few words of Turkish and I know how to say sword and dusk and stirrup. And now here we are, you and I, ready at last to start our pilgrimage to the dead man's tomb.'

'You didn't call him a martyr,' the young man objected.

'Look at the violinists and the harp players at Leicester Square tube station!' said his father. 'Look at the ragged poets wandering up and down Fleet Street, with no money as usual and desperate for a story, however false it might be; dear me, the art of telling stories is a pauper's job indeed.

No, I won't call him a martyr. It's nothing personal, it's just that he also had his faults; he was stubborn to the point of arrogance, so close to God that he started underestimating the power of the king with that typical disdain the ascetics have towards worldly things, and which to us simple sinners can at times be a little insulting, and that's still a fault you know; and look, look at the yellow stars in the violet sky, see how they fall back against the drive of dawn.'

'They shine very nicely in your chain mail,' said the young man.

'You know, I have my doubts about all the rigmarole of canonisation,' said the knight, 'but Thomas was a great man, and he knew how to die bravely, that's for sure, and it's the fortitude of the spirit on our journey that matters, as God knows, and not eternal salvation, which to me is a most intimidating concept.'

'The horses are thirsty,' said the young man. 'How much further is it to the Tabard Inn?'

'Not much further,' answered the knight.

'April is a beautiful month, and I hope the journey to Canterbury won't be as boring as I fear it will be,' said the young man as he scratched his head thoughtfully, made a sudden movement with his thumbnail and extracted a nit which he contemplated for a moment before speaking once again. 'Yes, I really hope not, but next time we come to London, father, please bring me in time for the Notting Hill Carnival. I'm still thinking about the archer and his choice of entertainment.'

'That archer fought at Crécy and Poitiers,' said the

knight, 'and reddened the meadows of France, and anyway he belongs to a different social class to us, and what he gets up to in his free time is his own business. But don't talk to me about a "next time", because that's in the future, and this is the fourteenth century, my dear boy, and you mustn't forget that life is a brief flame that consumes itself as unwittingly as this beautiful night that leaves us now in the face of the rosy drive of daylight. Look at the thatched roof of the Tabard Inn, look at that friendly-looking prioress with her double rosary standing in the doorway; it all seems rather worldly-looking, I would say.'

And they dug in their spurs.

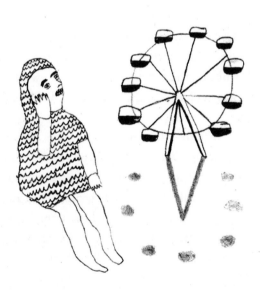

Gold and Guile

'Now, take a good look over here,' said Bluebeard. 'This is my wives' cupboard, it's where I keep their satin ribbons and their love letters and their books of Gregorian chants –'

'Wait, just hold on a second, what was that you said about love letters?' asked his fiancée, without losing even a fraction of the sweetness from her smile. They were holding hands in the middle of the gallery, lit up by the late evening sunlight, while on the other side of the window Bluebeard's warhorse was grazing peacefully, the fleur-de-lis painted on its saddle.

'I mean the letters they wrote to their many lovers,' he said. 'They used to like gossiping, and making fun of me because of the colour of my beard, you know, and even though I always told them it was genuine and not dyed, they never believed me. One of them went so far as to suggest I should take part in a publicity campaign for a Paris-based brand of hair dye, and another one insisted I should donate it to the Louvre so they could exhibit it in the worst possible place imaginable, damn it, nothing less than inside that blasted pyramid of such questionable taste, and, well, what can I say, that was a bit much, frankly. The little minx had even gone and signed a contract behind my back for an absolute fortune, and told the world about it until she'd spun a whole web of schemes around me which have made my life a misery, I'd be lying if I told you otherwise. My spirit has been scarred for too long now by an excess of betrayals, which at last have been happily softened by your affection, and so it feels like a dream to have found you, a dream come true. And while we're on the subject, tell me you love me, because it's hard to tell if one is really loved when one has power beyond the common man.'

'Is there anything else you want to talk about?' she replied with an almost imperceptible tone of impatience. Now only the pecking of hens in a nearby yard broke the solemn silence of the castle. And he blushed a little, as if struggling to confess a secret.

'Yes,' he said at last, 'I write music. No, nothing Gregorian, for heaven's sake, of course not! Rather more worldly things, things you can play on a lute under the window of a lady like any lover worth his salt. The Gregorian thing was the wives' idea, since for some reason they all ended up developing a fierce vocation for the convent after a while, and they used to ramble on about the triumph of the spirit over the flesh whenever things began to turn sour, and then beg me to let them go away to become nuns; but by then it was too late. But you're different, you truly are. There's only one thing that I would really hate, and that's if you weren't curious; I'm sick of women who only pretend not to be, and pretended virtue seems to me such a horrible vice. All I want is to share my life with somebody who is genuinely attracted to me; a man has the right to a little bit of peace of mind, at least from time to time.'

'Please, won't you tell me about how you fought alongside Joan of Arc against all those ferocious English soldiers?' asked his fiancée. 'And how the leopards on their banners trembled in the air of the battle, and how you laid siege to the white-walled town of Orleans?'

'Ah, she was a real woman, you know,' he answered, and sighed sadly. 'I remember as if it was yesterday that I saw her arrive at Chinon, so young and graceful amongst all those useless courtiers, and I saw her pick out the dauphin from the crowd with that combination of innocence and sheer nerve that only genuine chosen ones ever really possess. There was something about her which marked her out for an early death, something sublime and completely incompatible with this quagmire of a world. Yes, she was a real woman, and certainly difficult to forget, but then that's how cruel death is; death likes to demean itself, to appear to put itself in our hands so as to make it seem that its arrival is up to us, and so avoid being overcome with tedium in its never-ending dance over this flimsy scaffold that we call life; and so it always comes across as clumsy and capricious, and snatches away the best of us before we would say our time is up –'

'Sorry, I hate to interrupt your philosophising,' she said,

'but your horse seems to have gone without leaving any trace other than a large pile of dung in the middle of the lawn.'

'My squire must have taken it to the blacksmith for its monthly checks,' he replied with a reassuring smile. 'It has gold-coated nails in its shoes, you know. After all I am the Marshal of France.'

'And what else is made of gold in this house?' she asked. And Bluebeard cleared his throat, and looked down at the floor.

'Oh, not much, only the coat hangers on the wall of my study,' he answered in a dull voice. And while they spoke of trivial matters to do with the formalities of their approaching wedding, they went down a flight of stairs that smelt like the hold of a shipwrecked galleon and walked through rooms in which she saw for the first time that mess of boar's heads set in sulphur and coats of arms hacked to pieces with an axe and musketeer boots filled with Turkish gunpowder and unpacked boxes of Gobelin tapestries and manuals entitled *Alchemy for Beginners* and bat skeletons kept in jars of Bohemian crystal, and then they went out into the garden to watch the sunset. The sun looked like a bleeding giant lying on the sharp knife-edge of the horizon.

Bluebeard sighed.

'I like this hour of the day,' he said, looking at the sky, 'when the evening lights change colour and disguise themselves like imps, a world away from the dull routines of humans estranged from magic.'

'So, was she really a real woman?' she asked.

'Hold on a minute,' he replied, 'so you *are* curious then?'

And then he saw a pair of scissors in the pocket of her Karl Lagerfeld dress and asked her what they were for.

'Now who's the curious one?' she said. 'And it's not a very manly defect to be honest. Why don't you just carry on looking at the moon, it looks almost blue now over the fields.'

'Is blue your favourite colour?' he asked her.

'No,' she said, 'no, it's not. My favourite colour is red. Blood makes the world go round, you know that. Human history is written by the strong overcoming the weak; life isn't a fairytale, after all.'

And he nodded silently in agreement, scratched his beard, brushed a speck of dust from his peach-coloured velvet breeches and started to quietly hum the first few verses of the psalm *De Profundis*. And she hid the scissors more carefully inside her pocket and smiled, a little sadly.

Spain's Pain

'I will call it Spain,' the Indian chief declared, 'because it's clearly a very strange land; everybody likes pouring their hearts out in front of the TV cameras, and nobody speaks English.'

And after he had said this he walked right into the country followed by his men, and soon they were approached by a man with an outrageous beer belly.

'I'm the director general of a football club,' he told them, 'and if you agree to play for my team I'll give you silk shirts worth one thousand dollars like the one I'm wearing.'

And then a man with an iron prosthetic nose came up to speak to them.

'I'm an artist,' he said, 'and if by any chance you happen to have some revitalising powders hidden in your luggage you can call me any time of day or night on this telephone number.'

And then they were approached by a woman with a snakeskin handbag over her shoulder.

'I belong,' she told them, 'to a radio talk show devoted to investigative journalism, and I would like to know who you sleep with, what is life like without sex aboard three caravels, and why do you speak so quietly?'

The Indian chief didn't answer these questions and he carried on walking with his men following behind until they arrived at a city and saw a group of politicians queuing outside a restaurant and talking on their mobile phones about forest fires and tax agencies and traffic jams while one of them crawled around on the pavement looking for his American Express card. And the Indians walked impassively past road works and casinos and stalls selling inflammable plastic flags, and after a while they arrived at a wide open space where they sat down to rest, opened their rucksacks and took out their hamburgers.

'How long are we going to stay here?' asked one of the Indians, after a long silence. 'They're strange people – they don't seem to have gods of their own and they won't accept ours.'

And the chief rummaged in the pocket of his coat and confessed that he had lost his compass, that someone had stolen it outside the restaurant while he was watching the politician crawling around on the pavement.

'It'll be dark soon,' said another of the Indians. And they were all looking up at the sky when a waiter appeared with his tray at the ready announcing that they had to pay a supplement because they were eating on a terrace without realising it.

'Look how beautiful the moon is,' said one of the other

Indians quietly, 'it's as silent and sad as our moon. Let's follow it.'

And they stood up and walked along the copper-coloured path that the moon had opened up for them in the darkness, and they were never seen again.

The Ship of Fools

'That's the church of Sainte-Chapelle,' said the helmsman, 'with its fifteen stained glass panels and the rose window with images of the Apocalypse, and over there is the castle of Fontainebleau; both monuments feature in the history books and the tourist guides. Take a good look everybody, it's worth coming up on deck to see them, it really is a magnificent city.'

It was cold, but little by little they all came out and huddled together, clumsy and numb with cold, shivering in their rags against the October winds.

'I can see some beautiful women in the harbour,' confirmed a madman with a pencil behind his ear. 'They stand out for their famous sense of style, a little intimidating in how closely it follows the accepted norms of beauty, just as we heard they would be before we set off. And what can I say about the river? It's wonderful to see it so wide and majestic and so pleasant to sail down.'

'I remember Antwerp,' said another madman while he

polished his astrolabe, 'and that German painter with the long hair drawing pictures in the port; he waved to us and promised to send us a self-portrait.'

'I remember Lisbon,' said another madman who was wearing a portrait of Spinoza stuck to his head like a kind of hat, 'with its mapmakers and people selling cod.'

'Ah, the Portuguese,' said another madman with a book on quantum physics under his arm, 'always so painstakingly nostalgic about their age of discoveries; they take refuge in the past without tormenting themselves trying to prolong it, since they've had the good sense to cast off their imperial delusions; still, however beautiful the cities are that we've seen, I think we do well when we decide never to disembark.'

'A ship full of madmen wouldn't get permission to disembark anyway,' said the helmsman; and he took a poppy out of the pocket of his frock-coat and held it to his nose with the gesture of a poet.

'I remember Alexandria,' said another madman, his fingers stained with ink. 'When I first saw it I thought about all those books lost amongst the marble and the jellyfish, and all that science of demigods lost to us forever.'

'Better that than to leave it in the hands of sane people', the helmsman objected. 'Look at the Pont Neuf and the statue of Henri IV, a great king of France, lads, a man of action who knew how to win the love of his countrymen.'

'Or of quite a few of his countrywomen, at any rate', said another madman, before collapsing into hysterical laughter.

'Yes, that was more his style,' said the helmsman, 'but the

important thing is that to mention a name is to see the life of the person it belonged to, it really is. To speak of the king is to see him exploring the sighs of a woman behind a tapestry in the Louvre, to taste the wine that he drank from silver cups, to hear the whinnying of his horses at dawn when he rode out to hunt through the woods and the marshes; and also to see his sudden amazement when he found himself stabbed by an assassin, and to tremble at the sound of the murderer's screams as the torturers' irons pressed against his skin. A succession of images and feelings pass through the world with the determination of an unstoppable machine. And all the while the city changes, its buildings collapse, its occupants disappear like puppets in a street theatre; man is the only creature who doesn't realise he is mortal. Ah, the burden of thought! The lost images capture our imaginations and then disappear for ever, leaving us nothing to do but to describe them in the past tense. But then who cares about all that, my friends, when we're sailing down the wide Seine!'

'I remember Prague,' said another madman.

'But we've never been to Prague, you idiot,' said another madman at his side. 'You must have dreamed it, or maybe you heard somebody talking about it before we set sail.'

'Well, maybe,' said the other madman, 'but let's not argue about it because in any case Prague sounds good to me, it makes me think of cannons and musketeers and conspirators and Baroque towers, and its name alone sounds better than most modern music.'

'But then music nowadays is an absurd industry which

demands that you have to be famous before you can even put your talents to the test,' said another madman as he threaded a needle to mend his waistcoat.

'Why don't you keep your opinions to yourselves?' said the helmsman, before going back to eagerly breathing in the fragrance of the poppy; 'I know we've been travelling for a long time, but I remember Charleston with its gallows in the port, and that bustling slave market, and the traders chanting patriotic hymns amongst the barrels of cotton and cages of howler monkeys.'

'Why are we here?' asked another madman, who had been silent up until that moment. And some of his companions turned to look at him as if they'd never seen him before.

'You're getting dangerously close to sanity, and I regret to have to remind you that we are outcasts,' the helmsman replied sharply. 'Look at the dome of Sacre Coeur, look at that pair of lovers sitting in the old Citroen DS, they look so charmingly démodé, they could be posing just for us.'

'Yes, we're definitely outcasts,' said another madman. 'I remember when we signed that manifesto against political correctness, and when we all stood on board shouting that literature had become the vice of amateur journalists, and when you said that *Big Brother* was a programme of imbeciles who inadvertently speeded on the destruction of the world while an evil presenter drugged them with cups of *bitchyssoise*.'

'Did you live in Paris before you were mad, by any

chance?' the madman with the pencil behind his ear asked the helmsman.

'People throw their lives away queuing for the cash machine and in the unemployment offices,' said another madman, 'and in the waiting rooms at the quack's, and at Enrique Iglesias concerts.'

'Yes, very true, and remember that he was already famous before he became a singer, and clever marketing did the rest of the work,' said another madman. 'I think the best thing is not to get too angry with the world and to remember Callao, with its ruins of Colonial architecture, and those charming Peruvian fishermen, and the donkeys loaded with empty sacks of gold, and the policemen asking us if we spoke English.'

And the helmsman turned to the madman with the pencil behind his ear.

'No,' he answered, 'I won't tell you if I lived in Paris because that's a personal question. But look, all of you, look at the students in the boulevards talking about beauty under those reddish-coloured trees, red like the beards of the Danish pirates, like the pubic hair of the Irish fairies; autumn really is a state of mind. Look at the revolutionaries going to the cabarets of Montparnasse to talk about the meaning of life.'

'Who knows where we'll go after Paris?' asked a madman. And he looked up at the clouds. 'The truth is they're travellers too,' he said in a faraway voice, 'wandering and fragile.'

Tuscan Confidences

'Sometimes I think I don't really care much about painting,' he said.

And she looked at him, surprised, and took a few seconds to answer.

'My husband is convinced that you and I look alike,' she said finally, while she looked for a way to move ever so slightly so that he wouldn't even notice as she tried to find a more comfortable posture on that damned hard stool.

'Painting is like making mirrors,' he said. 'This canvas is like a window opening onto an abyss which I fill with your face to stop myself from falling in.'

'Wait a moment,' she said, 'what do mean when you say you don't care much about painting?'

And before she could finish the question they heard the shouts of the demonstrators who, crushed together in the middle of the Ponte Vecchio, were yelling at the top of their voices: 'Down with the Middle Ages! Bring on the Renaissance!'

And Leonardo went over to the window and looked out to see a juggler in moss-green stockings leading the crowd in the direction of the Duomo, while skilfully managing to keep half a dozen tomatoes moving through the air without dropping a single one.

'Look at me, all of you,' he was proclaiming pompously. 'What you see here are genuine American tomatoes; the Indian women smear their juice on the inside of their thighs in that land across the seas, a land of beaches warmed by an indolent sun who always forgets to leave the sky on time, and jungles even more luxuriant than the gardens of the cardinals of Rome, and deserts so wide and remote that the echoes of the papal anathemas that darken our lives would never cross them; they would drop down lifeless on the way like thirsty, starving ghosts.'

And Leonardo sighed with an indulgent smile and closed the window to let the silence back into the room. Then he turned to her thoughtfully.

'Well,' he replied, 'the times only change up to a certain point, if you see what I mean, and it can be quite amusing to see how human history is just a relentless pendulum that carries on regardless of our longings and our protests. But I get bored watching the cyclical nature of things, and I would really rather be an inventor, I'd find that much more fun. I imagine men balancing on their feet on top of a wheel that spins on a lute string, or fixing wings made of cigarette paper to their shoulders before jumping from the roof of the university building and making fools out of those stupid academics who could never imagine a life without dogma.'

'Hey, what's that you're drinking while you paint?' she asked him.

'French wine,' he replied, 'from the Loire region. Last night I dreamed I was in Amboise, and saw men hanging from the castle towers, and I heard the king of France asking me for new recipes for his cooks, and then I was trying helplessly to get up from a meadow of recently mown grass where I'd lain down to rest.'

'What else would you like to invent?' she asked him.

And he picked up his paintbrush again.

'I don't really know,' he said. And for a moment he turned to look with an expression of uncertain disgust at the bundle of sketches of cannons and corpses piled up on the oak chest next to the map of Tuscany and the copper candle-snuffer. 'No, I don't really know. Most of the time the things I end up drawing are completely different and far more extravagant than the idea I started out with, because my mind moves much faster than my hand, if you see what I mean, and most of my ideas shatter in the air before coming to rest on parchment. And they stay scattered forever in the air, elevated to the category of ideas that will always be secret and inaccessible to the speculations of future generations which, as you can imagine, I couldn't care less about; why should I care what people who won't even be born for centuries say about my work, people who anyway will be inclined to rambling and mindless opinions? No, I really couldn't care less.'

She was looking at him in silence and Leonardo felt encouraged to carry on talking.

'I'm much more interested,' he said, 'in studying those

mountains that I'm painting behind you, which hide people at the limits of my perception. I see a haughty-looking *condottiere* riding at the front of his men and his flags as they head into exile, disillusioned with the lies of war, and a mad, naked poet climbing amongst the crags armed with a golden sickle, and a lonely sentry sleeping on the battlements of a ruined city wall, battered by the winds of oblivion. The *condottiere* has blue eyes and is carrying a Milanese sword; the poet believes he is being chased by a band of crows who are screaming his name; and the sentinel is dreaming that a woman is posing for a painter while she tries to change position to make herself more comfortable.'

'I'd like to go to France one day,' she said, 'and walk through Paris in the light of the perfumers' towers, and wander through the galleries of the Louvre amongst groups of disdainful courtesans.'

And his face turned suddenly serious.

'Oh you will,' he said, 'you will; but be quiet now because I'm trying to fix that mysterious smile of yours once and for all. Your husband is right, by the way; maybe my theory of the mirrors was just one more invention and we simply happen to look alike by pure chance. Who would have thought it? It turns out wise husbands aren't an extinct species after all in these tempestuous times.'

And when she heard this her smile faltered just a touch.

'Ah, how the devil did you manage it, that's perfect', he exclaimed. 'Don't move, that's just what I needed!'

'What's cigarette paper?' she wanted to ask him, but seeing him suddenly so enthusiastic she decided not to and she sat on in silence.

The Secrets of War

When he finally stopped breathing, his iron breastplate stopped weighing so heavily on him and the blood sliding down his skin stopped being a slippery reptile and became, like everything else, a simple symbol of indifference, and that was when he realised, now that all of life's sufferings were behind him, that he could understand the language of birds, because two crows were standing on his face talking nonstop as they set to work filling it with holes.

'It's always the same old story: they celebrate their differences with cannon fire, get mixed in all this chaos of smoke and mud and flags and end up destroying themselves along the way,' said one of them as it pecked through his nose. 'It's all very well talking about the strategic intelligence of Egmont and Coligny and a hundred other captains of one religion or another, but at the hour of truth each man has to fight for his own skin, and ends up buried under a chaotic avalanche of oblivion. There's no cure for human folly, that's for sure.'

'I used to know this one,' said the other crow, 'his name was Ulrich and he was Swiss. I used to spend days watching him as he went about his routines in the camp, and I got quite fond of him. He was the playful type. I saw him telling jokes this very morning before the battle, and turning up the ends of his moustache because when he saw his wife again, in goodness knows what village in the canton of Berne, she'd like to see him with all his body pointing upright – or at least that's what he said to his friends and they all fell about laughing. I heard him sing as well, while he tightened his belt and prepared his harquebus, he had a nice voice.'

'And nice eyes until a moment ago', said the first crow with a bloodstained beak. 'But the beauty of the world is only transitory, and the laws of survival are far older than you or I. Let's get a move on, I can't stand all this shouting.'

Psalms and Piracy

The pirates climbed on board the *Mayflower* in the middle of the night while the pilgrims were asleep, grabbed the lookout by his arms and legs and tossed him into the sea before he even had a chance to say amen.

'Well, well,' said the Captain, 'I don't suppose you're hoping to spread this Puritan nonsense of yours over the lands of America. God knows what trouble you'd be capable of stirring up over there.'

And the pilgrims stretched and yawned with the cautious, childlike slowness of people who would rather believe that they were still asleep and dreaming, and they looked at the Captain for the first time in the crisp light of dawn. He wore a diamond nose stud and his fingernails were painted a stormy blue and he was stroking his double-barrelled pistol as if it were a fragile Lombard violin while he told them that now they would be working for him.

'This boat is certainly better than ours – I would guess it's at least 180 tons – so come on now, all hands on deck, this dead calm is just what we need, and we've no time to lose; after all we all know that the devil finds work for idle hands.'

And during two days of sweat and hard labour the pilgrims were forced to install the pirates' cannons in their boat, and to clean them and load them until they were ready for inspection, and then the excited Captain gave the order to hoist the Jolly Roger. And then, with the boat ready for blood and gunpowder, its new owners sailed it towards Bermuda and dropped anchor at Saint George where they recruited half a dozen jolly young kitchen girls who were fond of sunbathing on the aftercastle, and then they headed in the direction of Hispaniola and bombarded Santo Domingo until the sky over the town was left the colour and texture of orange peel. Then they set a course for Portobello, and looted the house of the Governor of Panama and stole his ebony chest full of royal dispatches with the seals still unbroken and old Spanish coins which were shiny and smooth from having been stroked so often with the persistent touch of greed, and then they set sail for Havana, where they allowed themselves the pleasure of attending a masque in the palace disguised in the pilgrims' clothes.

'My goodness, you look marvellous!' the other guests told them. 'Those darling black hats will be all the rage here this winter!'

And while they danced *sarabandes* and *gavottes* and helped themselves to punch with a silver ladle, the pilgrims spent the whole night huddled together in the hold, dressed like on the first page of Genesis and turning their troubles over and over in their minds. And so they went on with their fears and their sleepless nights, taking refuge in a constant silence that was lost in that boat swarming with wild words of looting and drunkenness and clapping in irons and slitting of throats.

And then one day the Captain turned to them as he polished his jars of cinnamon and cloves by the light of a small lamp.

'You've had enough fun for now,' he said. 'It's time for you to dedicate your time to the boredom that you had pencilled into your schedules and which, the more I think about it, the more I think you deserve. Yes, really, I've changed my mind; look, the island of Manhattan is over in that direction, look over there, you can easily make out the lights of Times Square in this grey November sky.'

And the Captain nodded to his men and they launched a large raft overboard and helped the pilgrims into it, where they sat with their eyes closed reciting a succession of monotonous psalms in Dutch, and the Captain himself threw down to them a big pumpkin pie which the kitchen girls had made for them.

'And you wouldn't even look the poor girls in the face because you thought they were a bunch of sinners,' said the Captain a little resentfully. 'Although I did catch you giving them the odd furtive look from time to time, which I'll say no more about, we're all only human after all. Here you go, here's three bottles of rum and a couple of turkey drumsticks, and my very own copy of *Ars Amandi*. Heave ho, off you go!' And as they rowed away he shouted after them: 'You could at least say thank you!'

And then he turned around. 'I don't like the name *Mayflower* for a boat,' he murmured.

'What about *Titanic*?' the boatswain suggested.

'Even worse,' he answered, 'it sounds too pompous, too English.'

'Maybe *Challenger* then?' said the boatswain a little nervously.

'By Calvin's horns!' roared the Captain. 'Will you stop saying ridiculous names and do something useful, like passing me my telescope?'

The boatswain stayed silent for a moment, thinking things over before he spoke.

'Now they'll go out and furiously reaffirm their beliefs,' he said. 'They won't tell anybody their secret but they'll take their revenge on their new country; they'll rely on the existence of evil so they can have someone to punish in the name of goodness.'

'Yes, you're probably right,' the Captain agreed in a faraway voice. And he carried on looking out to sea through his telescope, and frowned.

The Rogue and the Vihuela Player

Don Pablos woke up and looked left and right in the metro station corridor. He saw the posters for Iberia Airlines and the San Isidro fair and the Swiss pills that help you to sleep without any dreams and the Madrid Council for Social Affairs which covered almost all of the white, urine-stained tiles and he got to his feet, rolled up his polyester sleeping bag, tucked it safely away in his corner under the poster for Spanish Pop Idol, walked to station exit and went out into the morning air. Out in the Puerta del Sol he hailed a taxi and gave the driver the address of the school where he had to go to register for the public sector examinations for the post of 'Picaresque Rogue' which he had seen advertised a few days earlier in a government bulletin.

After almost twenty minutes of sharp turns and plentiful swearing, he saw the red and yellow flag hanging from a balcony.

'This is it,' he said, and he walked in through the door, passing a caretaker dressed as a rear-admiral arguing with a road sweeper about the official measurements of a football pitch. Don Pablos went up to the first floor and found himself faced with a long queue of sullen-looking applicants looking somewhere halfway between resigned and indifferent and, when he realised that they were all talking about the official bulletin as if they knew it by heart, he decided to launch a counter-attack against such a display of confidence with the help of a simple lie.

'I've got a letter,' he said, 'a letter of recommendation from Don Francisco de Quevedo y Villegas, Lord of Torre de Juan Abad, Knight of Santiago and celebrated poet.'

At this, a young man dressed in traffic-light-green sportswear and a horrible pair of sandals turned and looked his way.

'Well, worse luck for you,' he answered in a rasping voice. 'Quevedo's in disgrace, mate; and anyway he's a nobleman and has nothing to do with the 'Picaresque Rogue' business, where each one of us has to make a life for himself in whatever way he can. There's a reason why we are where we are, and Madrid is where the king lives.'

And Don Pablos looked out of the window and saw a young woman sitting on some stairs in a town square, with a needle in one hand and spoon in the other, surrounded by a flock of mutilated pigeons.

After a while his name was called and Don Pablos walked up to the enrolment desk.

'Sign here and come back next week,' the secretary told him, and Don Pablos signed.

'So, you're from Segovia,' she said, 'and your father was hung in public for thieving.'

Don Pablos bowed his head and nodded.

'Make a note of that in Section Eight where it says "other qualifications",' she said.

'Really?' he asked, blushing bright pink. 'I didn't know that. Thank you!'

'You said "thank you"!' she said, surprised. 'That sounds so old-fashioned!'

Don Pablos left the school and tried to get back to the Puerta del Sol by foot since he had spent all his money on the taxi, and he realised that the driver had cheated him by taking a roundabout route along remote, bumpy side streets, and Don Pablos thought to himself that he still had a lot to learn about being a rogue. He decided to take a walk and started wandering aimlessly through the back streets of Madrid. He saw a policeman standing to attention in the doorway of the Santa Cruz Palace, outside a limousine with dark glass in its windows and the star of Texas on its licence plate, and he saw some Singaporean tourists in the Plaza Mayor listening in amazement to the angry shouts of the waiters: 'No, no, no, on this terrace there are no complaint forms'; and he saw half a dozen artists protesting outside the town hall demanding state subsidies for the water in their swimming pools. And Don Pablos, who was starting to miss the quietness of his metro station refuge, went down into an underpass to clear his head and saw a man with a short blond beard sitting on a folding chair and playing the vihuela very beautifully.

'That's *Variations on Keep Safe My Little Cows* by Don Luis de Narvaez!' said Don Pablos, delighted.

The musician nodded. 'And what is your name, good sir?' he asked.

Don Pablos bit his tongue before answering. 'I could lie to him,' he thought, 'he seems like a nice man and it would be good practice if I could threaten him and take his money; after all I'd be doing him a favour by teaching him to steer himself a little more carefully along the hard paths of this world, and from this day on he would never underestimate the value of cunning.'

And Don Pablos was pondering these things and trying to decide what to do when he suddenly realised that his mind was no longer his own; it was being reeled in by the beauty of the music like a goldfinch caught in a net on its first flight out of the nest. And suddenly he began to have a strange vision, which at first felt alarmingly like the dizziness that comes after drinking bad wine. But then, with a rush of emotion he made out the shape of a woman in a white apron picking aubergines at sunset under a sky heavy with copper-coloured clouds, and a bloodstained horseman, with a broken sword at his belt, dismounting, exhausted, from his horse in front of a ruined castle, and a young woman with long black hair and cheeks smeared with carmine walking over a stone bridge bathed in the dull light of an oak wood. In the distance he could hear bells tolling from the tower of a hermitage, and the shouts of small boys playing on the banks of the Eresma in his home town of Segovia, calling him by that name which he had just been asked for and which, unlike everything else, had been saved from oblivion and now trembled anxiously in the air, as if one day it too could be wiped away, and no longer belong to anyone ever again.

And Don Pablos stood in silence as he tried to think of an answer, and he quickly, furtively wiped his eyes with the sleeve of his jerkin. And then he grabbed his dagger and looked behind him to make sure that he and the vihuela player were alone.

A Polite, Neighbourly Chat

And he took off his hat and bowed politely.

'My name is René Descartes,' he answered, 'and what might yours be, my good sir?'

And the elf said, 'I'm the elf that lives in your garden, and I have been for the last 156 years and, well, I already knew your name, to be perfectly honest; my friends and I usually say Renatus Cartesius when we talk about you because we think it sounds better but in the end, this is Sweden, and you know how we love our formalities here.'

'It's not the formalities that bother me about this country,' said Descartes, 'it's the cold.' And he had barely finished speaking when he let out an enormous sneeze.

'Bless you,' said the elf. 'You're here as a guest of the queen, aren't you?'

'Yes, that's right,' Descartes replied.

'Ah, the queen,' said the elf, 'she has such a passion for knowledge. It's a good thing as far as I'm concerned, and no doubt good for the general welfare of the country.

We're already better off than a lot of places. I mean, look at England with that crazy bunch of puritans who think they know it all; if Cromwell had his way, we elves would be sent to work in factories making chastity belts. Look at Spain, where the king's just married his own niece, you can imagine what kind of a monster we can expect to come out of that alliance; not to mention the never-ending and, to be honest, rather tedious complaining of the Spanish who are always clamouring for more money and going around with their prayers and processions in the hope that rescue boats will arrive from across the sea with a cargo that will free them from their debts and allow them to carry on living with the same old-fashioned airs and graces; but then I supposed everybody has their own obsessions. The fact is, our queen is an interesting woman and at the end of the day she does a good job, although Sweden is too far out of the way for her, and sooner or later she'll end up travelling off to some other country where she can have more of these intellectual friendships that she enjoys so much –'

'Excuse me, but did you say 156 years?' asked Descartes.

'Well, yes, give or take a year or so,' said the elf. 'This has been our garden for a long time now, and so we do get quite curious when we have a rational neighbour.'

'But the Swedes are very rational!' Descartes protested.

'Well, yes they are,' the elf agreed, 'but you're a foreigner, and we don't see many of those; I was talking about having a neighbour who was foreign and rational at the same time, if you see what I mean. Once I saw the Turkish Ambassador crossing the parade ground of the palace; he was wearing a dark green turban and a scarf made of mink, and I remember he had a big moustache, and also that he was very fond of the ladies. The local feminists kicked up a big fuss about that because, as you know, men from the South still have these old fashioned and completely unfair fantasies about northern women and, well, you can guess the rest. Another time I saw a pair of merchants from Tuscany in the port, they were very lively and pleasantly wild and disruptive –'

'Please excuse the interruption, but I suppose you must go abroad yourself from time to time?'

'Yes, of course,' said the elf, holding back a knowing smile because it wouldn't have been polite to seem patronising, 'of course I do. Sometimes we all get together in a wood somewhere in Prussia or Alsace or Moravia, and we have a little honey mead and some nut biscuits and some illuminating mushrooms, but it's getting more and more difficult these days because there are always new paths through the woods, full of soldiers on horses talking about the division of Germany and royal engineers pompously drawing up new maps and ordering more ditches and trenches to be dug. And on top of all that there's always the risk that some bumbling peasant will stumble across us sooner or later, whatever precautions we take to avoid it, and the poor deluded creature will end up thinking he's had some sort of life-changing experience, which as you can imagine is all very tedious, and what with all this going on we tend to travel a bit less these days.'

'Well, yes, religious wars are the curse of our times,' said Descartes a little hesitatingly, as if he was only speaking out of politeness while trying to think of something better to say.

'Not really,' the elf disagreed. 'Religion and wars have always gone hand in hand. But anyway, I wanted to ask whether you were writing anything at the moment?'

'Nothing much,' said Descartes. 'All I really do now is talk for hours with the queen from about five o'clock in the morning, and we knock back a couple of vodkas in the middle of the class with the scarlet Stockholm sky blazing in through the window; and I really am impressed with the towers of this city, and those long nights which leave the horizon racked like a battlefield, like a challenge to the mind, and those blond philosophy students with the long legs and the serious expressions who ride around the parks and bridges on their bicycles.'

'Do you think you'll stay here long?' asked the elf.

'I think about it sometimes,' said Descartes, 'but I doubt it.'

Some Words of Warning

'Right,' said the piper, 'from this moment on you're free and you can go wherever you want. That road leads to Amsterdam, with its red-brick towers and its coffee shops and its Moluccan artisans. And over there is the road to Belgrade, which at the moment is surrounded by Turks camping outside its walls with a huge army, and you'll see the yellow tents of the sultan and the smoking cannons inside the city walls, and the glinting of sunlight reflected in the blades of the scimitars.'

The children were very quiet so the piper carried on talking.

'Or you could go to Tangiers,' he said, 'and drink mint tea and study poetry; you could also go to Poland if you like, but I warn you, religion still has the attraction of rebellion there and there's always a chance you might end up as altar boys. And you could also go down the great Russian rivers and play at being pirates in the middle of those vast plains battered by cold, rebellious winds from the steppes where the nomads live. You could go to many places in fact, and no one anywhere will ask you about Hamelin.'

And then it started to rain.

'I'm cold,' said one of the children. 'I was cold before I left the city and now I want my scarf and my umbrella.'

'I'm hungry,' said another child. 'I want a slice of black bread with mustard, goat's cheese and Thuringian sausage.'

'I'll get bored without my computer games!' cried a third child.

'Freedom is a heavy load,' said a fourth, 'and soon we'll want some order in our lives, and you should know that because you're an adult.'

And the piper stopped looking blankly at the rain drops darkening his green laced boots, and turned the empty pockets of his purple breeches inside out.

'Well,' he said, 'I'm a travelling artist, and it's not easy to make a living in these rationalistic times, you know; it's as if magic has become some kind of third-rate rubbish, as if the whole world prides itself on having an opinion about absolutely everything, however stupid it might be. And don't forget either that your parents were so mean that they wouldn't even pay me a sum equivalent to 15,000 old Euros; but every problem has a solution. If you'd rather stay with me and you want me to entertain you then I'll tell you the story of a knight who, a long, long time ago, galloped into a thick forest with his lance at the ready to rescue a queen who had been taken prisoner.'

The piper paused to make sure that he had everybody's attention.

'Ah,' he said with a sigh, 'you really should have seen him. He wore a crest of eagle feathers in his helmet, an emerald on the hilt of his sword, and an amethyst on both his spurs, and he was riding a handsome Hanoverian horse with a white mane.'

'Where is the knight now?' asked a child.

'He belongs inside a book,' said the piper, 'and only comes partly back to life when somebody opens it.'

'That's a literary destiny,' said another child, 'but we want something different now that we've left everything behind to follow you.'

And the piper put on a serious face.

'Well, aren't you ambitious!' he said. 'You can't escape destiny, in whatever form it comes to you.'

'So tell us what happened to the knight,' asked another child. And they all sat down on the grass to listen to him, no longer caring about the rain.

'The queen had been kidnapped and turned into a tree by a wood sprite,' the piper explained, 'and the knight had to find that exact same tree, and to do this he had to rush with his lance at one trunk after another in the hope of finding her and returning her to her former appearance.'

'What happened?' asked another child.

'He's still looking for her,' replied the piper, 'striking randomly at trees without ever stopping to rest.'

'He'll find her one day though, won't he?' asked another child.

'Probably not,' the piper replied. 'By the way,' he added, 'you could also cross the wide ocean and explore the lush tobacco fields of Virginia and hear the sound of the whip cracking through the air and see the red-skinned Indians queuing to buy barrels of rum at crossroads which aren't yet found on any maps.'

But the children had stopped listening.

'Is it really true then that children's stories can be as cynical as adult stories and have an unhappy ending?' asked another child with a very serious expression. 'Can queens really be turned into trees on the whim of a spiteful wood sprite, and become invisible to the rest of the world without ever being heard of again?'

'Yes', said the piper, 'without being seen or heard of ever, ever again.'

'And can something so cruel happen to just anybody and not just to queens?' asked another child. 'I mean, disappearing and being turned into a tree and never being seen again?'

'Yes', said the piper.

An Attack of Nostalgia

James Samuel Hook looked at himself in the mirror, sighed deeply and carefully inspected the white feathers of his hat, his crimson dress coat with silver anchors on the cuffs, his Spanish sword, and his crocodile-skin shoes with the skull-shaped buckles, and then, without changing his expression, he took one last look out of the window at the lush spring foliage of Green Park, crossed the shadowy hallway and opened the door.

As he walked down the stairs he thought about his father, Archibald Hook, who had been abandoned by his men somewhere in the Spice Islands, and later rescued by a Dutch brig and who ended up setting up a tobacco and alcohol shop in Amsterdam which went on to become the centre for the best conversation in all the city. And he thought about his grandfather, Ethelbert Hook, who had gone down the Missouri river, admirably rejecting the charms of the Indian women, who were dressed like a capital sin, and who threw otter skins to him from the river bank while he bowed deeply to them like a true gentleman as he tapped out the rhythms of *pavanes* and *contredances* against the planks of the raft. And he thought about his great grandfather, Aloysius Hook, who, with one memorable thrust of his sword, had killed a peer of the realm in a duel over a disagreement about the superiority of Italian madrigals.

'And all this,' thought Hook as he crossed Piccadilly, 'all this long legacy of bravery just to end up wallowing in this sense of failure, in this never-ending bitterness of love, in this senseless and harmful fidelity. All this to get lost in a labyrinth of sorrow just because of a certain Wendy Darling from a middle-class family in Kensington, a scatterbrained little madam who wouldn't even know where to find Jamaica on a map and who had already given three snotty little brats to that pretentious Peter Pan, a yokel from the North American colonies who spoke with the seductive accent of the savages and drove her wild telling her fantasies about the exotic countries of the New World and saying he could fly like an albatross when really he could only lie like a slave-trader.'

And Hook crossed the street and took off his hat to two elegantly dressed ladies who asked him how he was managing on his own, and was he getting on with his memoirs, and what did he think of this most bizarre month of April, when the rain and the sun didn't take turns in an orderly fashion but instead both took their place in the London sky at once, as if the weather had gone quite mad; and all this without even mentioning that extraordinary rainbow which the city's amateur astronomers were examining from their balconies and their roof gardens with homemade telescopes and all nervously agreeing that yes, one could most definitely make out the shape of a boat right in its centre, anchored in a spiral of seven colours with the sails set and the Jolly Roger high on the mast.

'I know nothing about it,' said Hook. 'I know nothing whatsoever about any rainbow,' he repeated wearily, tired of hearing the same news day after day. And later, after taking his customary hot chocolate and reading his daily two pages of Horace, he decided to resist the temptation of solitude once and for all and to go up onto the roof himself. And he saw dozens of Londoners standing in their shirtsleeves, waving maddeningly at the rainbow and shaking their umbrellas like excited schoolboys and saying to one another, 'Yes, it's definitely a pirate boat, it's light and manoeuvrable, look at it closely, look at the canvas and the freeboard, look at its cannons and its topsails, look closely at its aftercastle and you can just make out some men running frantically around it, as if they don't know what to do, as if they're waiting for an order which never comes, as if they're begging for the return of their captain.'

And then Hook noticed that the whole city of London was beginning to look gloriously like a gigantic fruit stall, because the mild rain falling over it was coming down in many different colours. Drops of green water were falling on the hills of Hampstead, blue on the mansions of Chelsea, orange on the Houses of Parliament at Westminster, red on the Tower walls and the dome of St Paul's, yellow on the roofs of Southwark. Britain's capital had turned into a kind of brilliant, glittering jewel, with each district making up a different shining surface depending on the colour of the rain that had happened to fall on it. And Hook gritted his teeth and went down to his rooms and, without even taking off his dress coat, which was drenched in purple water, he sat down at his desk and grabbed hold of his pelican feather quill.

'Writing is an arduous business,' he thought, 'and memory is a rough and choppy ocean, blown about by unexpected winds which insist on being called memories too.'

And he served himself a glass of port, and after the first mouthful he dropped his quill in the wine and looked up at the faded and now almost illegible calendar hanging on the wall opposite the mirror, and he began to feel anxious.

Ireland's People

Two brothers were walking one night close to Kilkenny when one of them looked up at the moon and said that it looked like a sickle. The other brother looked up then and said that it looked like a lemon.

Scarcely had they said the words when the brother who had spoken first suddenly felt a terrible pain in his neck, and it began to bleed as if it had been cut by a dagger, and he had to knot a handkerchief around it to hold in the blood. And his brother began to cry pale, bitter tears which tore through his skin.

At that very moment a man happened to pass by on a black mare.

'Without a doubt,' he said, 'you must have come too close to the fairies who rule over the lands of Ireland; you must have said something to make them feel you were trespassing on their powers, since the art of naming things with a poet's logic belongs to them. This country of ours has had a hard history, and there are those who fear that one dark day even the fairies will end up speaking with a Piccadilly accent. Follow me to that house over there on the top of the hill and I will do my best to get you out of this predicament.'

And they did as they were told and went into the house and sat at a table on which were two tankards of bitter and a pot with a hawthorn branch inside it. Then they watched as the man went out into the yard, galloped away and disappeared into the night, and they began to fear that they had fallen into a trap. But the wound of the one and the tears of the other had dried up, and this gave them comfort, and so they began to drink the beer as happily as if they were sitting in a tavern.

And that was when another man appeared in front of them, older than the first; he wore a green three-cornered hat and had three or four days' worth of beard; on his belt he wore a double-barrelled pistol. The two brothers asked who he was.

'They used to call me Captain Freeny,' he replied, 'and for many a year I laid down my own law on the roads of this island. But one day I got too close to those I shouldn't, like you did today, and I held up a young man on his way to Dublin who went by the name of Redmond Barry. But how was I to know that he was under their protection; they are always so unpredictable when they decide on a new favourite? I aimed my pistol at him, he raised his arms, I took his bag and I rode away on his horse; barely an hour later the animal reared up and threw me to the ground. I sat up with surprise and saw that the pocket of my coat was blackened with blood, and there was nothing left inside it. I understood then that my luck had changed, and I got lost in the woods for the first time in my life, and also my last. That very night I fell into the hands of justice and a few days later I was taken up to the gallows at Kilkenny jail, so secretly that my men decided to keep my name alive and replaced me with an imposter who stole my legend, and now everybody talks about him as if it were me, something which saddens me but which right now is beside the point. And now listen carefully. My son brought you here to ask for a favour. That young man that I held up is now a gentleman known to all as Barry Lyndon and who is now down on his luck and friendless and his fate is looking bleak, as he too has been abandoned by his protectors since he went and made himself so English. Go and look for him and give him this pistol with which I snatched away his first fortune and warn him that terrible misfortune awaits him if he doesn't abandon his house this very night. And, if you do this, I can journey at last to the peace of the dead, whatever that might be.'

But the two brothers were filled with mistrust and they ran straight out of the house. When they arrived at Kilkenny, the wound had opened again and the tears were pouring out once more. The first brother made a hasty getaway; his trail disappears in Cork, where he was seen looking for a boat to America. The second brother lost the sight in his left eye and today makes a living telling stories on the roads of Leinster, and it was from his own lips that I heard this one.

Under the Danish Skies

Prince Hamlet got up from his rocking chair, looked sleepily out of his turret window at the Swedish coast and the Strandvej mansions with their landscaped gardens, yawned reluctantly, rubbed his temples, and quietly cursed his recent tendency to sleep for a little longer each day. He glanced at the front page of last week's *Berlingske Tidende*, abandoned on his desk next to the ship inside a vodka bottle and the pot of withered geraniums and the jar of valium and the empty inkpot, and he put on his Vivienne Westwood punk sunglasses, ready to go out.

He walked down the castle stairs like a sleepwalker, ignoring the ice-cold, musty water dripping from the ceilings and the scruffy-looking guards having a fencing match in the parade ground, and he unlocked his bicycle, which was chained to the drawbridge, and went into the city for his usual beer at Ophelia's, the topless club full of Swedish tourists who always urinated unsteadily against the walls of the underground car park before getting drunkenly into their Volvos and heading for home. And Hamlet sat at the bar, stroking his bottle of Carlsberg, which he always drank without a glass, and looked at Ophelia.

She had pretty eyebrows and eyes the colour of smoke and a husky voice, and when he came in she said, 'Hi Hamlet, how are you?'

'I don't even remember any more,' he replied.

And she went over to the gramophone, which was playing a scratchy, faraway recording of *How Should I Your True Love Know*, and she lifted the needle. Then she took a daisy with no petals from the pocket of her black leather skirt and started to stroke it gently.

'Well,' she said, 'here we are again, just the two of us in this poky little hole. Just look at you: an old fashioned gentleman who keeps sniffing from his mahogany and platinum snuffbox just to check that he's awake, who shakes the dust twice a month from the sixteen volumes of his unfinished encyclopaedia signed personally by his beloved Diderot, who never leaves Denmark –'

'Apart from that one time,' he interrupted, 'I went to Paris incognito, but I didn't stay very long. Yes, I swam naked from one bank of the Seine to the other and I fell asleep in the royal box in the opera house surrounded by first ladies, and I stole an hourglass from the supermarket in the *Faubourg Saint-Honoré*. But people were just too bothered about style in that city, frankly, they made me feel like I came from a country of lumberjacks,'

'Yes, yes, I remember,' she said. 'Now, tell me what it said in the *Berlingske Tidende*.'

And Hamlet started picking off the Carlsberg label piece by piece with nervous fingers.

'Well,' he answered, 'they were talking about me, for a change. They said that I'm a coward.'

And then the silence spread across the bar like a serpent that had just uncoiled.

'And now look at me,' said Ophelia absently, as if she hadn't noticed. 'Come on, make a real effort, look at me closely. I'm carrying your load, you gave me your pain because it was too much for you and now you feel lighter, don't you? Free from the weight of love, free to blame destiny with your tedious excuse of nostalgia. Look at me and my girls, we spend half our time sitting in the ladies toilet with our cheap little mirrors and our five kroner notes, snorting up another dose of insomnia –'

'Do you know what?' he said. 'It also said in the paper that there were wars in the world.'

She knew all too well the tortuous impulses behind those interruptions of his, like cardboard rafts trying to dodge a storm on the high seas, and she forced a smile.

'There's an opium stain on that black velvet bow tie you're wearing,' she said, 'and your waistcoat needs somebody to iron it.'

'What time do you shut?' he asked.

'At three in the morning, as usual,' she replied. 'So, tell me what kind of wars they are?'

'Wars over money,' he replied. 'There are cities full of soldiers who buy border maps from antique shops, study them closely with a magnifying glass, and then they group together into battalions, fix bayonets onto their rifles, put a blindfold over their eyes and march blindly day and night through the woods, searching for a battlefield where they can reactivate the course of history.'

'I don't see what that's got to do with money,' Ophelia objected. And Hamlet shrugged his shoulders with the exhausted gesture of someone who doesn't want to waste energy trying to explain things.

'Look,' he said, 'three o'clock is too late for me, I won't stay awake that long and anyway I don't have any change; I'll pay you another day.'

'You owe me for 132 Carlsbergs,' she said.

'I said I'd pay you another day,' he insisted.

'I said that you owed me something, Hamlet, not that I want you to pay me,' she replied with another attempt at a smile, as sad as the first one.

And he looked out of the window. 'What was that bird that dared to cross the heavy Danish sky?' he asked.

'A skylark,' she said. 'They sing so beautifully.'

'Wars for money,' he murmured to himself. 'I think I'll sign up as a volunteer.'

'Can you leave the door open?' she said. 'The club looks cosier from the outside. But wait a second Hamlet, Hamlet, you've left your dark glasses on the bar.'

'You keep them,' he said. 'With the way I see the world, I don't need them.'

Out in the street he kept his eyes on the sky, as if he didn't want to lose sight of the skylark's trail, and then he slowly dropped his gaze until he was looking at the floor and its shadows; its wandering, whispering, fleeting, fearsome, shapeless shadows.

One Hundred Years and Seven Minutes

The poet crept softly into the room, and seeing the princess asleep on her bed beside a dusty, half-opened copy of *Vogue*, decided to kiss her; and then things began to change one after another.

A crossbowman woke up at his guard post next to the dynastic banner high up on its tower, and the raven that had been pierced by his arrow and had remained suspended in the air for a hundred years and thirty seconds fell down dead in the moat on top of a mess of outdated mobile phones, faded Trivial Pursuit cards, expired packets of Dexedrine, and cuttings from leaflets about the Big Bang, which were rapidly turning the colour of fresh blood.

The king stretched apprehensively and looked closely at his face in the mirror, which was steamed up from the damp coming from the nearest window.

'A century is a long time,' he said irritably, 'and this kind of curse is the worst thing that can happen to a person.

Human time is difficult enough to bear as it is, but this twisted version is an absolute nightmare.'

And then he felt his bald patch, frowned, went over to the built-in wardrobe, took out one of his wigs and adjusted it on his head as best he could. When this was done and he felt a little more sure of himself, he started to walk around the room in a tentative manner which was meant to combine majesty with bewilderment.

'It's strange, I dreamed about revolutions,' he murmured dejectedly, as if he had little confidence in his new state of being a wide-awake king.

'That sounds like a prophetic dream,' said the poet. And he held back a moment before speaking again, as if worried about frightening them with too much alarming news. But then he decided it was better to tell the truth than to silence it.

'This kingdom,' he said, 'is now known as the "old regime", and the people from the neighbouring districts buy philosophy books from market stalls and shout about atheism being a basic need.'

And the king's fool woke up with a series of self-conscious yawns, and looked apprehensively at the little bells sewn onto his chequered hood.

'Honestly,' he said, 'I look ridiculous; I don't dare finish the joke I was telling about life and death before the enchantment because I don't suppose it'll be funny any more.'

The princess was sitting on her bed flicking impatiently through the beauty pages in *Vogue*. 'Daddy,' she said, 'I'm sure you wouldn't make me marry him just because he came in here and ... well, you know.'

And the queen woke up.

'Darling,' she whispered, 'this is just between you and me, but you know I wasn't exactly crazy about your father when I was promised to him for reasons of state a hundred and twenty-one years ago, but now I've learned to see his good points; he has a rather intuitive talent for foreign affairs, and doesn't snore any more. Goodness me! What is that racket coming from the parade ground?'

And the king opened the window and the poet and the queen went and stood beside him, and they all looked out to see the soldiers who had just woken up coming out of their sentry boxes and their garrisons covered in rust, rubbing their faces and their arms and pointing at one another as if they were all strangers.

'You all look ridiculous, frankly,' said the poet. 'These days weapons are intelligent and you might as well throw away those absurd old relics that are completely incapable of destroying the world and start looking in the arms dealer section of the Yellow Pages.'

The room filled with an intimidating silence which made them all feel awkward.

'What's that on your shoulder?' asked the fool, who was worried to see that nobody's thoughts were turning to humour, and as a husband and father was feeling increasingly uncomfortable at the prospect of being left without a job.

'It's blood,' said the poet. 'The royal forest is full of thorns which stick out through leaves covered in acid rain and, to be honest, nobody tries to go through it because they say it's impossible to cross.'

'My personal physician can help you,' said the king, 'and while he's at it he can give me some sort of pill to get rid of this headache I can feel coming on; somebody call my doctor!'

'Your majesty,' said one of the servants, 'Doctor Guillotine is still fast asleep and hasn't come out of the enchantment yet.'

The silence in the room was breaking like a window pane struck by a stone, and was filling with cracks through which came the increasing murmurs of the newly woken household. The queen, sitting on the floor, grabbed a pair of scissors from her sewing basket and started trimming her toenails. And the poet began to gaze at the paintings by Holbein and Van Dyck and Fragonard which were arranged chronologically on the wall according to the dynasty of the kings they depicted.

'Oh dear, nobody buys this stuff any more,' said the poet in a careful voice, trying not to shock anybody or to sound too pretentious. 'These days painters rely on critics to announce how talented they are at art shows and in the Sunday supplements, and that's usually enough to convince the masses.'

And then he saw the Shakespearian sonnets strewn across a mahogany bookshelf beside a bag of mothballs, and this time he couldn't hold back a humourless smile.

'Out of date again, I'm afraid,' he said in a quieter voice than before. 'These days writers dress in black in an attempt to hide the burden of their horribly ordinary features, and say that they feel persecuted by their characters, and other things like that.'

'My dear boy, why have you come here?' asked the king, who was beginning to feel frightened hearing about so many changes.

'I suppose, your majesty, that I was spurred on by an urge to travel,' the poet replied. 'I set out in search of simple things which contain, reproduced to scale, all the immensity of the world.'

'And how did you cross that wood if it's as impenetrable as you say?' asked the fool, without trying to disguise his bitter expression of mistrust.

'Well,' replied the poet, 'I'm not really sure. I can only say that at every moment I felt absolutely determined to carry on going. For a long time I'd felt fed up with the inconsistencies of poetry and I just needed a little completeness.'

'Hey, hold on a moment, don't look at me!' said the princess. 'I had a dream too: I dreamed that I was holding a clock with no hands and I heard voices warning me to throw it away and run because it was a bomb.'

And she let out a choked sob which moved them all.

'I think you've got the wrong idea about me,' the poet told her. 'Let me warn you right now that I won't demand or promise fidelity. We poets aren't easy people to pin down and we get distracted by every little thing that takes our fancy; and anyway, times have changed, love is a much more prosaic thing these days and men aren't expected to flutter around women any more trying to win their attention, in fact people look down on that nowadays.'

'Oh, really?' she said, smiling with surprise, and secretly feeling very curious. 'In that case come and sit over here and tell me about your writing, I'm sure you remember some poems by heart.'

'If you don't mind, I'd rather talk to you from a bit of distance' said the poet stubbornly.

And her face lit up with a sudden glow of princess-like fury.

'Daddy!' she said. 'Have you seen how this wretch speaks to me? And don't tell me it's not surprising, even if he is whole century ahead of us!' And she furiously ripped the beauty page out of *Vogue* and tucked it inside the neck of her transparent nightdress and glanced at the poet out of the corner of her eye. But by this time nobody was paying her any attention because at that moment the royal secretary burst, panting, into the room.

'Your majesty,' he gasped, 'all the castle telephones are ringing on our switchboard and it's a disaster because we just can't keep up. We've got the Dalai Lama on hold, and the Babylonian ambassador, and an arms dealer from California, and the accounts department from *Vogue*, who say that we have to immediately pay the subscription for a century's worth of issues –'

'Oh, damn it, all those beauty tips so stupidly wasted!' the princess lamented, shamelessly.

And then she switched her attention back to the poet.

'What's your name?' she asked without looking at him.

When she found that he was no longer at her side she rushed to the window and saw him sitting in the middle of the park with his eyes closed and his hands on his knees; and then she saw him slowly start to move and softly, stealthily examine a line of ants who were beginning to cross the grass. And she saw him blow on the hundred-year-old cobwebs that covered the rose garden, raising a cloud of incredibly fine, violet-coloured dust which vanished into the air like a genie released from its prison, desperate to hide itself by losing its colour forever.

And the princess went over to the queen with a conspiratorial smile.

'Tell me honestly, mother,' she said, 'is it true what you said before, I mean, about daddy and you?'

Valmont

As he watched Chevalier Danceny in discussion with his seconds in the middle of the snow, he felt something he had never felt before. He stroked the hilt of his sword with slow, tentative fingers and realised that he was about to be reunited with the hereditary art of his ancestors, which he had never expected to be of any use to him; the art over which the resonance of his name had been built and which he was returning to at last with the surprise of someone who realises that in the back of their memory they hold a sacred and undeniable lesson, with the relief of one who has rediscovered the idea of valour.

The touch of his sword was strange in its novelty. He looked at his fingers and remembered the thighs of women who had been deliberately cold before letting themselves be touched by him, becoming openly voracious once they felt liberated by the privacy of closed doors and satin sheets, between which they no longer called him 'viscount'. And a smile spread across his face as he compared those tempestuous, frenzied passions of the bedroom with the frozen trees of the Vincennes wood now separating him from Paris and the world.

He saw a cat crouched under a bush and assumed it must belong to one of the houses of *Saint Mandé* and had come out to hunt. He observed the stripes on its motionless fur and in a flash he was struck by the realisation that the cat, like all creatures, had its own lineage linking it back to a precise infinity; a succession of cats had passed on the baton of life with the inexorable discipline of those who, unlike him, had not been created to wallow in the luxurious geometries of seduction. And then he thought of two or three more things: a night spent in conversation with Chevalier Casanova, who advised him in frank, deliberate tones of the wisdom of moderation and of loyalty to the classics as dawn shattered against the three bottles of Bourgogne wine which they had managed to empty between them; a night-time stroll across the Pont Neuf when he had suddenly bumped into a man with a hard expression and a hurried pace with whom he had exchanged apologies whilst two women standing by the railings whispered that the lawyer Danton was in a hurry tonight; and the raggedly-dressed young woman who once met his gaze through the window of his carriage on his way to the woods.

Danceny's seconds looked like crows in their black frock-coats against the dense whiteness of the snow. He felt powerful and utterly exhausted.

Merlin's Exile

One day Merlin arrived at the court of the king of France.

'I'm a wizard,' he explained, 'and not long ago I decided to leave my island and travel the world to demonstrate my science.'

Seeing him there with his hair a mess and several days' worth of beard thinning his face, wearing an old Thomas Burberry scarf, a Salvation Army overcoat covered in multicoloured patches, a Pink Floyd t-shirt, black corduroy trousers with holes in the knees and suede boots caked in dried mud, the king and his court stopped dead in the middle of their *gavotte*, took off their gold masks to look at him more closely, and tried to intimidate him with their silence.

'Goodness me, a travelling Briton has come to visit us,' the king said scornfully, and a chorus of flattering giggles enfolded his words with the mistrustful, slavish discipline of those who are protected by privilege and splendour without feeling at all sure how long it is going to last. And

Merlin took an orange from the pocket of his overcoat, peeled it skilfully and a nightingale immediately emerged from inside and flew around the throne room to the sudden silence of the court, who all turned towards the king to wait for his response. And the king sat down on a marble step and began to stroke the head of his favourite greyhound.

'Look, young man,' he said, 'this is a country addicted to reason and my philosophers are busy tracing new lines on the map of the cosmos while your shabby compatriots persist in their habits of importing our wines and lusting after our women; go down to the royal kitchens, ask for something to eat, and then go away.'

'He must be a fool to call me a young man,' Merlin thought furiously as he roamed the paths of Versailles amongst the rustle of skirts fumbled secretly behind the geometric hedges, and the barely-concealed groans of Parisian courtesans, and the resigned gossip of the gardeners. 'What could they have been thinking of, that bejewelled bunch of idiots? Maybe I should have just told them outright; I'm not a young man, dammit, I'm just hopelessly immune to all the marks of old age and all I ever do is struggle to find a cure for this nostalgia for lances and harps and mists which makes my whole life a misery. It's terrible being a misunderstood genius; it's so hard having to watch other people's stupidity, especially when it seems to be becoming the norm.'

Then Merlin travelled to Spain and saw the king posing as a bullfighter for an arthritic sculptor while some of the courtiers formed circles to talk about actresses from the comedies, and others to play blind man's buff, and others to stare at the prime minister who was sitting in a corner polishing some castanets with a dirty rag on which you could still make out the national colours.

'Well,' said the king, a little glumly, 'let's see what you can do.'

And Merlin took a rook from a chessboard out of his pocket, and as he threw it into the air he set it on fire just by looking at it, and the rook became a flame and fluttered past the dismembered coats of armour and the second-hand mirrors and the adverts for the lottery and the slot machines out in the parade ground until finally it burst into a delicate rain of purplish stars which melted away as they touched the floor.

'Not bad,' said the king, 'not bad at all; but it's modern logic that we're after here, you know, I'm fed up with being told day after day that we need to become a more forward-thinking country.'

And at that moment all the bells of Madrid started ringing in unison and the king took off his bullfighter's hat.

'I know it's time for me to do something but I can't think what it is,' he said. 'Go and talk to the beggars at the gate and ask them to give you some coins with my father's picture on them; the ones with mine aren't worth much due to chronic public mistrust. Between you and me, I admit I find the economy a terribly tedious business, with all this jargon about devaluations and interest rates and suspension of payments. Oh, and try not to let them rip you off, they can tell you're a foreigner from a mile away.'

Merlin left the palace and soon he crossed the sea and arrived in Tunis.

'I'm a wizard,' he said.

'Only in Allah is all magic found,' said the sultan. 'But I'll see what you can do.'

And Merlin blew on one of the tapestries decorated with moons and letters and triangles that hung on the wall, and it turned into a flying carpet which, after flying out of one window and back in another, landed at the feet of the sultan with a white rose resting in its centre.

'Oh no, not another flying carpet!' said the sultan miserably. 'Where are you from?'

'I'm from Wales,' said Merlin.

'Ah yes, mountain people,' said the sultan, 'wild and brave if a little pig-headed; I've seen your rugby team a few times on my antique television; but anyway, now is not the time to start making observations which, to your depressed state of mind, might seem a little xenophobic. Hospitality is a law that I like to seal with a gift. I'm offering you a wide desert which you can wander about at your pleasure without anybody there to bother you.'

And Merlin left the fountains and towers of the sultan's palace and went deep into the desert and thought about the bright-eyed young knights errant who he had seen riding out to conquer the world when time was younger and there was still something worth searching for in the woods and groves which had been chopped down by the knife of oblivion centuries ago. He sat down by a shrub with grey-brown branches withered by the biting heat of the African winds and took out a pack of cards, laying them out neatly on the sand in a game of solitaire which he hoped to lose so that he could feel some unexpected emotion to relieve him from his obsessions. And so he began to turn each card until it was facing upwards, and he saw that one by one they all showed the ace of hearts. And then Merlin understood that he had forgotten the art of not playing tricks.

He looked up at the sky, stabbed by the quarrelsome blades of twilight. He began to feel cold, and he decided to smile.

Missing d'Hubert

Gabriel Florian Feraud finished putting on his old hussar boots, sat up shakily on the dusty floorboards of his bedroom, straightened his moustache and glanced at the collection of maps of Marengo, Austerlitz, Waterloo and Santa Elena lined up on the wall next to the rusty nail where his general's sabre was hanging. Then he opened the door and had to close his eyes against the honeyed evening light as he went out into the orchard to find his friends in their usual place, sitting around the low stone table in the shadow of the fig tree.

'Goodness knows what you dream about in those naps of yours, Gabriel,' one of them said to him.

'I don't need dreams,' Gabriel Feraud grunted, 'I have memories.'

And he looked at the three of them, one by one, as if inspecting the troops, and he thought that his face must look as decrepit as theirs did, that he too must look like a book whose pages had been turned too many times by the rough fingers of time.

'Do you know what? Spain was one big adventure,' he said abruptly, knowing how they liked to hear him talk about his days in the war. 'On the one hand I didn't like it because they were such lawless people, who seemed to rejoice in their own grime; such primitive ferocity didn't sit well with the neatness of our uniforms. We were trained to fight like gentlemen while they all seemed to have been brought up in slaughterhouses and couldn't tell the difference between a man and a beast. But on the other hand I liked them; they were brave by instinct, as if they didn't need to be trained in the art of valour.'

'Things didn't go too well for the French armies out there,' said one of his friends as he topped up the four glasses with wine from the Rhone.

'Life will always start going badly sooner or later,' Feraud replied, 'and I must say I hate the repression of civilians. I knew Murat was doing the wrong thing sending all those patriots to face the firing squad, and all these years I've felt sure that he dedicated a last, secret thought to them when he found himself facing the same fate. But they really were savages, nobody can deny that. I remember riding once at full gallop through the main street in Madrid when suddenly a woman appeared at her balcony and, fast as lightning, threw a flowerpot at my head which broke into a thousand pieces just a hair's breadth away, and no one in the squadron even stopped to look because we were all in such a hurry. And for a moment I imagined her going back into her dingy little house amongst the frying pans and tiles and vinegar thinking to herself, "I almost hit the Frenchie"; and then she would forget all about me because I was only a shadow in a uniform, a horseman with the order to kill. And that was the month of May, my friends, just like it is today. Blue skies, the fresh air of spring, which continues on and on in its cruel cycle and there's nothing men can do to change that.'

'In any case Spain wasn't the best posting for a soldier, and I know others who had a different kind of luck at that time,' said one of his comrades. And Feraud smiled.

'Oh, I know exactly who you mean,' he answered. 'No, he wasn't in Spain, and he wouldn't have survived it; he was far too meticulous, he always refused to go beyond the limits of the discipline. But please, not today, not today. I've told you a dozen times that all this talk about the two of us in a series of duels was quickly exaggerated along the marches and counter-marches of the war; conversations like that are perfect for killing time in the middle of the night while you're sitting around the campfire and the enemy is waiting for daybreak behind the next hill. I suppose he knows that I know where the money comes from that he sends me and, believe me, I don't feel humiliated, on the contrary in fact. I take it as a kind of bond between us in recognition of the dangers we shared in distant fields when the century was young and we were filling it with the scent of blood, but oh! my friends, the month of May. The month of May.'

Hope is Only a Virtue

They had become used to seeing him like that throughout the journey, gruff and withdrawn without being rude, and with his gaze fixed permanently on the sea. They couldn't know that the sea was new to him, that he'd never seen it before, that he had spent his whole life amongst hills and olive groves punished by a dry, lime-coloured sun.

And despite this they liked him. There was something attractive about that man with the sallow skin and bushy black sideburns who spent so much time leaning on deck, sometimes nibbling a gherkin soaked in vinegar, sometimes silently smoking his cigar as he gazed at the lines of the horizon as if trying to learn them by heart.

'Buendía seems like a man of character', they said. 'He's not the kind to give up easily, he's going to really be someone in America.'

They had got used to his ways and by now they paid him less attention. But that night was different for everybody and they could all sense a new excitement on board. There were just a few hours left before arriving at the harbour and unloading trunks and setting foot on the new land where they would stay forever; there was just a little time left before leaving behind the sea that had taken them from their homelands.

'Spain is on the other side of the world now, José,' said one of his countrymen who, like him, was hardened by defeats and narrow escapes. And Buendía nodded.

'You're right,' he thought, 'and it hurts to know that I will never see it or fight for it again; but now all of that is over forever. All the uprisings and repressions, cheers and chains, burning utopias and bitter revenges are left behind me; there will be none of that here. I'll arrive in America, I'll find a wife, we'll have a son and I'll call him Aureliano. And he'll be a happy man, a free citizen in a fair and prosperous republic. He'll grow up in a nation of hope where there'll be no place for resentment or corruption or slavery or firing squads. And he'll give birth to a long line of Buendías who will be innocent and happy, and gloriously oblivious to the cruelties suffered by a Spanish ancestor.'

And he felt tired for the first time that night. And they all saw the shadowy lines of the coast.

A December Day

'He's English,' said the deserter. 'You only have to look closely at him to see that air of self-importance, that look of an invulnerable gentleman who acts exactly the same wherever he goes, as if he can control any dangerous situation and come out without even a scratch.'

His companion heard him and looked briefly at the Englishman and then up at the grey, uninviting San Francisco sky.

'It's cold,' he said.

'It won't be so cold when we finally find that blasted gold that's going to make us rich,' said the deserter, 'and when we've got land of our own where we can build a big house, just imagine it, a far cry from wandering around on these stinking docks. But look closely, he's not travelling alone, I'm sure he's not; look at that strange servant following behind him, *he's* not English. And neither is that beautiful girl, I can tell you that for free, with that face and those clothes she must come from India or something. They make a strange trio, they really do. And they've got money, you can see it a mile off. Life hasn't been hard with them, my boy, indeed it hasn't, you can tell just by looking at them.'

'It's been hard with us plenty of times,' said his companion.

'But it won't be soon,' said the deserter. 'Soon we'll find that Californian gold that drives everyone who touches it crazy and we'll forget everything that came before, we'll forget all this waiting and hunger and tiredness. By the way, sometimes I think that things weren't so bad in the regiment, seriously.'

His companion looked at him with surprise.

'I mean it,' he insisted, 'it wasn't really so bad. Maybe it's my Welsh blood, I don't know, but the fact is that sometimes I start missing those days, and I remember special moments, you know, the kind of times you realise you'll never live to see the like of again. I remember once we were sitting around the fire in the middle of the night singing *Garry Owen*, when suddenly we were interrupted by the howl of a coyote, long and trembling like the stab of a blind assassin. There were thousands of stars in the sky, and we sat looking at them in silence for some time, and then we carried on singing, but a little quieter now, looking at the shadows on each other's faces. And then I realised that we hardly knew each other, that behind each face was a mysterious history, hiding the traces of dusty villages and bottles of whisky and the lips of young ladies and the crossing of roads, my boy, the crossing of rivers and deserts and borders which ended up with us all coming together in that godforsaken regiment in exchange for a miserable salary and disgusting rations of beans and lard. But there we all were, carrying our lives on our backs, and it was a special moment. And there were more of them, oh yes, there were more. I remember another day riding at sundown, with the setting sun hitting us in the face like an explosion of glory, as if the trail of dust our horses were leaving behind them was about to wrap us forever in a cloud of mystery and pluck us out of this world, as if we were about to become part of a picture book. Yes, I remember it well. And I don't need to add that I remember *him* too, he was a great character, you have to admit it.'

'Well,' said his companion, '*he's* not looking for gold in this land, that's for sure, or wandering around the docks of San Francisco like we are. I wonder what the hell he's up to right now.'

'He'll be giving an apple to his horse,' said the deserter, 'or sitting on a chair with a blue cloth in his hand, polishing his sabre and his spurs, or looking at himself in the mirror with that domineering face of his, saying, "George Armstrong Custer, you and your regiment will make history in the United States army."'

'I heard he's stationed in Kentucky now,' said his companion.

'Yes,' said the deserter, 'it seems they've put him in charge of keeping an eye on those crazy Ku Klux Klan people. But he won't like that, he wants some real action. And anyway, who cares what he's doing at the moment, my boy? The world is just a big ball of fire spinning through the air at high speed, and those of us who live on it count for nothing because we don't last long, and then others come along and talk about life as if they've known it forever. What does it matter? I just hope we hurry up and find that gold so I can go around in a carriage as fine as the one they've just loaded the Englishman's luggage onto. Just look at him, he's so full of himself.'

The carriage started moving and Phileas Fogg passed by very close to them for a moment, without noticing their presence.

'Yes,' said the deserter, 'a great big ball which we slip around on according to the will of destiny. You can cross the sea to China, or you can look back, back towards the east, to all the dusty American roads that you and I travelled down with bullets and hard labour, and which that arrogant gentleman is about to cross, I presume, in the opposite direction, tucked up in a comfortable train which you and I can't afford to pay for. What a life this is!'

His companion wasn't listening to him.

'Yes,' he said, 'he's a real character, no doubt about it. Maybe he's looking in the mirror, like you said, thinking, "George Armstrong Custer, in some valley, on some mountain, there's an Indian calling up his gods and waiting for you with a weapon in his hand."'

And they both stood in silence, watching the hustle and bustle of the docks. A gust of wintry San Francisco wind swept up their words, wrapped around them and carried them across the world, over seas and frontiers and abysses, as if unsure whether to drop them before they faded away, to let them fall at random on some stranger who would hear them without understanding them. The gust of wind passed over a wood in China, where a man was carving his lover's name into the trunk of a cherry tree; it passed over the Tartars' steppe, where a shepherd was sleeping beside a hooded eagle and a dead wolf; it passed over the city of Krakow, where a young orphan named Josef Konrad was celebrating his fifteenth birthday by forging plans to cross oceans he had never seen. The gust of wind stopped there for a moment and then carried on travelling, weaker now, before disappearing forever.

The True Story of Bob Dylan's Shadow

Bob Dylan had just got back to his dressing room and put a towel around his neck, with the shouts of the audience still audible in the distance.

'Hold on, where's your shadow, Bob?' asked his guitarist.

'What do you mean?' Bob Dylan answered.

And the guitarist frowned and refused to back down.

'Look, I saw you two together just a moment ago, just before you came in ... hey, I know what's happened, dammit, it must have got trapped on the other side of the door, you didn't give it time to follow you in.'

Bob Dylan looked at himself in the mirror with a pencil in his hand and said nothing, and the guitarist climbed out through the dressing room skylight onto the roof, took a detour across the back yard, retraced his steps along the corridor towards the dressing room door, and then there it was: Bob Dylan's shadow. He recognised it at once, it was definitely him, that messy hair, that nose, that harmonica, that leather jacket, those boots.

The guitarist was about to say something but at that moment the fuse blew on the neon tubes lighting up the ceiling, and the shadow's profile didn't change but its content did. It began to flicker, pale yet defiant on the floor, as a series of confused images spread across it like a slow dream, filling the shape without spilling out of it. The guitarist saw a train track crossing immense wheat fields surrounded by a wire fence that had turned the colour of rusty copper under the glow of a dipsomaniac moon, and he saw a collection of carnival masks hanging from a mandolin string, and a black woman sobbing on the porch of her house, and a man stationed behind a wall with a rifle with a telescopic sight. He saw motorways lined with fairies with wild hair and scars on their faces trying to flag down a car so they could escape to somewhere else, but all the drivers were passing them by with their headlights switched off while the stars in the sky spun mechanically like a garish, broken-down Ferris wheel with the prices of a ride written in the air. And the guitarist also saw words, thousands of words wrapped in Virginia tobacco, humming like crazed insects and trying in vain to break out of the limits of the shadow, and he had just crouched down to try to read them when the voice of Bob Dylan interrupted him from behind the door.

'So, is it there?' asked Bob. 'Come on, tell me, did you find it or not?'

And the guitarist answered that yes, it was there.

'Well, let it stay there for a while,' said Bob, 'until I start to miss it.'

Weltschmerz

Little Red Riding Hood went into the wood.

'Oh, you again,' she said when she saw the gloomy, haggard-looking wolf sitting with his arms crossed under a walnut tree. 'It's hard work always having to greet somebody who insists on looking so mournful all the time. I suppose you're going around again in one of those depressions of yours, obsessing over the changes in the food chain and punishing your stomach drinking that insipid nettle soup at midnight like some kind of a penance.'

'And you,' he replied, his voice thick with resentment, 'I suppose you're off to visit your grandmother, since we all know the current state of German macroeconomics, with those Berlin politicos railing against extravagance and threatening everyone with the imminent collapse of the welfare state; and with all this on the political horizon it makes sense to have someone in the family who can pass down some hard cash. And let's not fool ourselves at this stage in the day; no one can deny that elderly people like to ease their old age by believing their family really loves them with disinterested affection.'

'You know,' said Little Red Riding Hood as if she hadn't heard him, 'I could just sit down here with you for a while and share a swig or two from the bottle of cherry brandy I'm carrying in my basket Grandma wouldn't notice.'

And so they did, and on the third mouthful the wolf, who was less hardy than Red Riding Hood and who with age had become overly fond of sweet liquor, started getting drunk and saying that nothing in the world was as it used to be, that the moon had lost the sacred, metallic power of its mysterious beginnings and now just seemed to creep dutifully around the sky, and that all the old terrors of the forest had disappeared without a trace, as if they refused to live in a world run by an illiterate mob, and that motorways were springing up everywhere full of hunters packed into Toyotas and Land Rovers.

'Have you ever thought about emigrating?' she asked him.

'Yes,' he said, 'to the South; to a warmer climate, maybe to Spain.'

'You can't be serious!' she protested. 'They're terrible with animals! Look what they do to the bulls. They put on a big party just to watch them bleed to death while everybody cheers, for God's sake! And I've also heard they throw goats from the top of church towers. And I've even seen photos of greyhounds being hung in a wood; honestly, I can understand cruelty but not barbarity.'

'England would be worse,' the wolf objected. 'There's no

wolves or she-wolves left there at all, and they'd take me for some kind of totemic apparition and give me nothing but trouble, not to mention how lonely I'd be there.'

'Loneliness is everywhere all of the time,' said Red Riding Hood conclusively, as she put the bottle back in her basket and took out a cup and two dice. 'Will you play a little game with me before I go?' she asked, and he said yes.

He threw the dice first and got a seven, and then it was her turn and she rolled eleven.

'You always win,' he said, 'and I'm sure you cheat.'

'My dear friend,' she replied, 'I'm not responsible for history; it's an old question of chancellors and margraves and prince electors who have always only needed to give the order for a whole army of musketeers to rush out and put an entire village to the sword without anybody ever caring about the dead. My grandma, who's as old as the wood, could tell you some terrible tales about fires and looting which she's seen with her own eyes. I have to be able to survive by myself and I need to be clever; but a game is a game and you have to know how to lose. Anyway, get a move on and come along with me for a while, I've wasted enough time here with you and it'll be dawn soon, and you know how scared I am of the light.'

'Oh, yes, of course,' said the wolf, politely.

And he started to walk along beside her, and she pulled down her hood until it almost covered her eyes to protect herself from the growing daylight.

'Little Red Riding Hood,' said the wolf, 'what prominent, shapely hips you have!'

And she didn't answer.

'And what enticing, luscious lips you have!' he insisted.

And she carried on walking without saying a word.

'But your eyes are cold and threatening, despite your youth,' he said gloomily.

'That's because of my contact lenses,' she said. 'I get tired eyes because I spend the whole day reading fairytales.'

And the wolf looked serious and asked her why she did that.

'Well, for no reason in particular,' she answered, 'but you can hardly expect me to start reading the *Frankfurter Allgemeine* with all that news about commotions on Wall Street and tantrums in the Brussels offices and hurricanes devastating hungry countries and the referee's latest mistake in the Bayern versus Borussia Dortmund game. Seriously, the world is falling to pieces and I don't want to know about it. It's hard enough to have to admit that everything you've been complaining about is true; the old magic has left us to our fates, and the wolves have been stripped of the symbolism they had before an avalanche of centuries and ugliness left them poor and neglected like so many other creatures who once found a refuge in poetry and now find themselves freely profaned by a growing army of yobs. That's just the way things are, and there's no point fooling ourselves that there's some way around it. Do you know what, wolf? I think this global deterioration has something to do with the twisted German destiny. In this country there's an unspoken, latent fear that perfection, if we finally achieved it, would become unbearable, so we're secretly relieved when we see it contaminated by widespread evils that make us feel just like everybody else and keep us away from Promethean temptations.'

'What do you learn from fairytales?' the wolf asked a little uncomfortably, as if he'd rather change the subject.

And Little Red Riding Hood put on her poker face.

'Well,' she said, 'if I had to sum it up in one phrase I'd say this: various tricks of a practical nature. And now I think you'd better get away from here because I can see those men coming quickly this way, the ones with partridge feathers in their green hats, camouflage waistcoats and high rubber boots. Believe me, I brought you here for your own good, you're out of shape and you'll be an easy target any day of the week if you carry on doing nothing but sitting under a tree thinking about the evils of the world; you could really use the exercise.'

And the wolf ran away and she sighed, a little annoyed with herself. She had her doubts about him.

Tristanshout

Tristan de Leonnois sat in the doorway of the bookshop drinking brandy, and he started to stroke the brim of the glass.

'For heaven's sake, Tristan,' said the bookshop owner, 'you're forty-five years old, you can't just sit there all day complaining about missed opportunities and messing around fixing string instruments!'

'I'm not that bad,' Tristan replied, 'I'm just putting the final touches to my harp and then I'll be ready to set out and become a travelling musician on the roads of Brittany, and warn all the young men against the perils of love.'

'Just because Isolde has her own slot now on BBC2 presenting a feminist chat show on Friday nights, that doesn't mean you can let yourself go like this,' the bookshop owner insisted. 'The world goes on turning, you know.'

And Tristan put the glass on the floor and looked down at his dark green corduroy doublet with the *Free Brittany* badge on its sleeve, his old Spanish leather belt, his black stockings and his shoes with the copper buckle.

'It's not that,' he said. 'It's just that time seems to me like an open window which lets in ferocious hurricanes.'

'Yes, yes, whatever you say,' said the bookshop owner, 'but you should go out walking a bit more around Saint-Malo instead of spending hours sitting here staring up at the clouds like some kind of oddball. Last Tuesday I saw a group of tourists staring at you and whispering and getting out their Polaroid cameras; on Wednesday the police came round twice asking after you; on Thursday an ambulance came from the Breton Mental Health Service; and on Friday it was that chubby doctorate student from the University of Dublin. Listen to me, will you, and at least try to act normal. Why don't you take a walk along the city walls? This is a historical town, you know.'

And Tristan stretched out his hands and looked at his fingernails.

'I think art has the answer,' he said. 'I'm composing a poem about boats with a dragon's head on the prow, and a crew of men armed with doubled-edged axes. The boats row against the wind towards an island where the cliffs are lined with silver and the people don't know how lucky they are.'

And the bookshop owner felt curious despite himself, and sat down beside him.

'Well, then what happens?' he asked, gruffly.

'I'm not sure,' Tristan replied. 'I think the invaders lecture their captives about the necessity of violence, drug them with mead, seize their women and then, as soon as they set sail with the women on board, their boats are swallowed up by an avenging storm, one of those storms that represent the cyclical nature of the disasters that befall mankind. But it's a long poem and I never find the time to finish it.'

'Or your harp either, I notice,' said the bookshop owner, irritably. And he lit his pipe, stood up a little unsteadily and wandered over to the counter to sell a second-hand copy of the Odyssey to an Indonesian customer who first looked at the two of them, then at the 'No Smoking' sign and the poster of the forest of Brocéliande and the portrait of Dylan Thomas and the chestnut umbrella stand and the marijuana planted in the Sevres porcelain flowerpots, and then stayed quiet for a moment, frowning and looking confused, before finally leaving the shop scratching his head.

'I'm going to be an inventor,' said Tristan. 'I'm going to design a flying machine and launch it with a few drops from that Holy Grail I bought on the black market in Rennes and fly it all along the Breton coast up to Normandy, and then fly it inland towards Paris and Aachen. It'll be in the shape of an enormous bird, with seats finished in silk and I'll call it Tristanshout, because it'll be a shout of loneliness, a symbol which will provide refuge for the dreams of all those poor troubadours who have suffered from the pains of love, all those who have had their hearts pierced by the memory of a cruel muse. And so, with my harp in my hand, I'll play my music as the machine carries me majestically through the skies, and I'll see all the peasants looking up at me saying, "Look, there goes Tristan, isn't he talented?"

'They'll be too busy working the land to look at you,' the bookshop owner objected. 'Not everybody is a poet, you know. I don't live off poets, in fact you're my only poet customer, and for a while now I've been thinking of closing and setting up a souvenir shop. But of course, you couldn't care less about that. You just sit there with your head full of never-ending harp music. It's as if the words of us poor mortals were just a distraction from those ever-changing visions of yours; today it's pirates and shipwrecks, yesterday it was knights in shining armour riding all night under an orange moon, and the day before that it was vultures circling over the London palaces. And so it goes on day after day: swords buried up to the hilt in deserts of lava, elves leaving their woods forever in the middle of a raging fire, druids wrapped in chains suffering the humiliation of a foreign circus; and a whole host of other miseries which I can't remember right now.'

'There's going to be a storm,' said Tristan. 'I can see lead-coloured clouds coming from the west.'

'Tristan, by all the devils of Avalon, you never listen to me when I talk to you!' the bookshop owner protested.

'From the west,' said Tristan.

The Best Kept Secret in Greece

Aphrodite was smoking her usual six o'clock spliff, sitting alone on a cedar wood bench looking out at the calm sea, and she glanced at her nicotine-stained fingers and the wrinkles on the palms of her hands. After taking the last drag, she stubbed it out on the back of the bench, poured herself a drop of Cypriot wine, and sighed.

She knew her sighs had once been powerful enough to make even the most hard-hearted sailors cry out in anguish, change course and forget about their wives, but now she sighed softly, as if restraining herself, and she stood up and walked barefoot to the edge of the water, where she saw a wretched-looking castaway.

'You must be the goddess Aphrodite,' he said.

And she knew she would have to explain to him that she was fed up with seeing her anonymity constantly under threat, and was longing for the peace of oblivion, and didn't want to be named by anyone.

The castaway sat up and looked at her, quite unabashed.

'I'm from Brooklyn,' he said, 'and I've sailed to this island to tell you that your cult has been declared officially obsolete. The word and the world have been Christian for centuries.'

And Aphrodite slowly ran a finger across her forehead and cheek and down to the edge of her lips, and she threw her orange Kashmir shawl over her shoulders and asked him to follow her up the hill towards her whitewashed house with its moon-shaped windows and its wide terrace presiding over the big-bellied sea, where a peplum made of Cretan linen and a pair of white Calvin Klein knickers were hanging on a washing line, drying in the late evening sun.

The man had lost some of his initial swagger, and was beginning to look a little uneasy. Aphrodite invited him into her room and made him sit on the floor opposite a hamper full of fresh lemons, and a packet of Rizla paper, and an old jar of blusher and a biography of Botticelli.

'So, what's Brooklyn like?' she asked, out of politeness.

'Oh, nothing special. The most interesting thing there is the museum of the caravels,' he answered. 'They arrived one day loaded with armour and horses, and nothing has been the same since.'

'And how did you find me?' she asked.

'Ah, well, I heard you sigh,' he said, looking even more uncomfortable.

'And what are the women like in Brooklyn?' she asked, and then he grimaced.

'They buy self-help manuals in the shopping malls,' he

answered. 'Manuals about euthanasia and husbands who are addicted to television.'

'What does "husbands" mean?' she asked.

'What do you do in your free time?' he replied.

'What does "free" mean?' she asked. And then the man looked up at the ceiling and sighed with frustration, and Aphrodite frowned.

'These days the world is full of mortgage loans and satellite dishes,' he said, 'and you've been forgotten, nobody remembers that you're still here being who you are and that the true cult belongs to you.'

And the man stood up, looking relieved to have got that off his chest, and he had crossed halfway to the door when he turned around and asked her how he could travel east without losing his way; he wanted to carry on travelling around the unexplored world through deserts and gorges and mountain ranges and, with a bit of luck, forget about Brooklyn and never go home again.

'Sooner or later you'll go back,' she replied.

'I think I'll stay for a while in India,' he said. 'They say that you can find peace and love there.'

'Peace and love, peace and love, what nonsense! You can only have one or the other,' she murmured, trying to control her rising temper. And she closed the door, went into her bathroom and turned on the hot tap. And as she waited for the bath to fill she went to the window and leaned on the sill to enjoy the last rays of sunlight still trapped in the branches of the olive and almond trees, like warriors in a holy battalion ready to perish in the fight against a giant, overwhelming aggressor, like the dying embers of a once powerful bonfire now choking and vanishing in the poisonous freshness of the air.

And Aphrodite turned her head thoughtfully, wondering if these small pleasures were the privileges of age. She crossed the room and discovered that her jar of moisturising cream was empty and tossed it scornfully in the wastepaper basket, and then she climbed naked into the bath humming *As Time Goes By*. Once in the bath, she grabbed hold of her exfoliating glove, tilted her head back, closed her eyes and started to massage her thighs slowly, very slowly, and she knew that this time there wasn't a single dead cell floating in the water.

Brain Drain

'Damn!' said God, 'Not another secondary school teacher! Stand to one side please and wait there.' And he looked at her briefly. She had hairy cheeks and was wearing a locket, containing her eldest son's wisdom tooth, over her housecoat.

'What subject do you teach?' He asked.

'Literature,' she replied.

'Really? How interesting!' said God. 'Perhaps you could recommend a book for me to read?'

'My husband is a cardiologist,' she said, 'and I take paddle tennis lessons twice a week on our upmarket housing estate.'

God sighed and reviewed the situation. He had finally answered the prayers of the Spanish and agreed to come down to their country to sort things out, since nobody else had ever managed to do it however many times they'd tried.

'Listen,' he'd told them, 'I'm making an exception here,

and I'd rather word didn't get out about this because I don't want to offend anybody, although I have to say I'm a little fed up anyway with the French and the way they always look down their noses at me.'

After giving them this warning, God had decided to give each one of them an appropriate profession. A young girl arrived with a pleasant face, blonde highlights, and a pair of expensive leather gloves folded in one hand, and God asked her to say 'orange juice' and 'seat belt' in English.

'You will be an air hostess,' he announced.

Then a man jumped in front of God dressed in a hood with little bells sewn onto it, with seven poisoned daggers on his belt.

'What do you believe in?' God asked him.

'Audience ratings,' the man replied.

'You will be a television producer,' said God.

And then a small boy appeared with a serious face, weighed down with a rucksack full of books, maps, compasses and pencils.

'I'm sorry,' said God, 'you'll be unemployed, I'm afraid, but social security will look after you for a while and there's always a chance you'll get a grant to study abroad. What's more, to make things a little easier for you, I'm considering declaring the suspension of envy as a cardinal sin in this country as a deterrent, although I haven't quite made up my mind about that yet.'

And then there was a great commotion and God saw a group of artists burst in.

'We don't want to be what you decide we should be,'

they said. 'We possess the gift of creativity and we want to be writers, painters and screenwriters, and we want to be treated as an industry.'

They were all wearing large wooden spoons around their necks, and were nudging and winking knowingly at the television producer and calling him by his first name.

'Do you know what,' said God, 'I didn't get the chance to tell you before but the fact is that I've just invented this talentometer which you see here, it's completely foolproof, of course, that goes without saying, and I have to admit I'm particularly proud of this one, hold on a minute, where are you all rushing off to?' he called after them as they ran away in a panic. 'Well I never – I don't remember the last time I saw anyone run that fast,' said God.

And then he turned back to the secondary school teacher who was looking at him through her thick glasses with an expression which was part vacant and part alarmed.

'Surely *you're* not frightened of the talentometer?' God asked sternly.

'What's talent?' she stammered back at him.

The Truth and the Masses

'The emperor's naked,' said the little boy. And everybody became completely still, as if an old master of logic had touched them with his magic wand, as if the whole city had turned into a glass cake. But then, little by little, the first voices were heard.

'Well, when you put it like that,' said the emperor's concubine angrily as she folded up her vulture-feather fan, 'you might also have said that he's an awkward lover, and prone to eccentric fantasies which I won't say any more about, unless someone pays me the right kind of money. And also that he has a weak character because of an outmoded idea of power which he finds just too overwhelming. And also that he's obsessed with inspecting his private zoo every single day as if he doesn't care much for human company. Just yesterday I looked out of my window and saw him talking to an elephant and feeding him peanuts in hollandaise sauce while that ridiculous pair of swindlers, who *we* all saw through right from day one, spent the whole day snipping in the air with their scissors in the upstairs room, as if the entire kingdom had gone completely mad.'

'When you put it like that,' said his geometry professor, tucking an unfinished crossword inside his tangerine polka-dot frock-coat, 'you might also have said that he prefers to ignore the fact that the apex of the social pyramid collapses if the base isn't firm, and that houses of cards don't last forever, and that there are certain unstoppable historical processes.'

'When you put it like that,' said his chief marshal, shaking his monocle, 'you might as well have said that we need to invest far more money into our arms industry for it to continue to function and to preserve our prestige as a nation, since it's been two months now without a word about us on CNN, and the president of the United States recently confessed that he wouldn't know where to find us on a map of the world.'

'Well, there's no need to read too much into that,' said the emperor's concubine. 'If we started letting ourselves get depressed about the North American president's lack of general knowledge, we'd all end up breaking into the pharmacies.'

And everybody watched them in silence as they talked, standing completely still in the street strewn with a carpet of white roses and guarded every fifty feet by a soldier standing to attention with a bayonet fixed on his rifle.

'When you put it like that,' said a lady selling fish, 'you might as well have said that he needs to get some exercise. His majesty has got himself a bit of a belly now, and he has to stay handsome these days, when everything's controlled by the basic principles of political marketing –' She saw the little boy who had first spoken looking very serious. 'Hold on, what's wrong with you?' she asked.

'Well, nothing,' said the little boy, 'it's just that I wish I'd just kept my eyes closed before speaking, but I'd made a bet with my classmate about the universal value of truth, and now look at the mess I've made, and I suppose it's too late to sort things out.'

'Ha! That's a good one! And why should you have kept your eyes closed?' asked the emperor.

And then everybody turned to look at his majesty and saw him sitting with his hands crossed primly below his navel, while the courtiers carrying his train kept firmly straight faces, as if proud of being able to hold back their laughter with such little effort.

'Let's see, young man, what can you tell me about your musical tastes?' asked the emperor.

'Well, I like Mr. Mozart,' said the boy.

'What do you know about him?' asked the emperor.

'Not much,' said the boy, 'only that he used to travel a lot and things didn't turn out very well for him.'

And the emperor looked exasperated.

'When you put it like that,' he said, 'you ought to realise that partial knowledge is a dangerous thing which has to be handled with as much care as a Meissen tea set, because saying an isolated truth is not such a simple thing, you know; the world has been saved many times over by the things we don't say. You'd have done better to just calmly whistle any passage from *Don Giovanni* instead of deciding to play the virtuous innocent here, in front of everybody, ruining my evening as if I didn't have the right to enjoy a personal secret, Goddammit, as if the position of emperor held nothing but obligations. Well, that's just not true, a thousand times no; I confess I've had secret exhibitionist tendencies my whole life, ever since a crowd of tutors were imposed on me when I was your age, and the only thing they knew was how to repress impulses. And today I simply wanted to feel the warmth of collective admiration without having to think any more about how stupid people are. Oh come on, for crying out loud, don't give me that face. It's part of my job to sing the praises of my people, but that doesn't mean I can't really see what the world is coming to.'

When the emperor had finished speaking there was silence for a moment, but it didn't last long.

'I read *Hell-ho! Magazine* every Thursday,' said a voice from the crowd.

And then many different voices rang out one after another, each one a little louder than the last, saying, 'I don't like Chaplin' and 'I don't like Van Morrison' and 'I think Sharon Stone is really classy' and 'I once fainted at a Ricky Martin concert' and 'I can't wait until Sunday so that I can spend all afternoon dunking chips in ketchup and looking in the shop windows at shopping centres' and 'I've called in a few times to ask the TV fortune tellers to predict my future' and 'I won't leave the house without my socks and sandals'.

'Now do you see what I mean?' said the emperor. 'What do you want to study when you grow up?'

'I think maybe political sciences,' said the little boy.

'Well, there you go,' said the emperor, 'I suppose that today you've had your first lesson.'

And as soon as he'd said this, he stretched out his arms and tensed his biceps like a bodybuilder, looked at his concubine and stuck out his tongue.

By Satellite

The spaceship landed on the moon sixteen minutes late and stayed still for a moment like an exhausted insect, with its *Osborne Bull* sticker and its *Made in Brussels* label fixed to the hatch. And finally the astronaut came out slowly and started to climb down the ladder, and took his first clumsy, rather hurried jumps on the moon.

'This is one small step for mankind,' he said, 'but one giant leap for my autonomous region.'

'Where the hell are the flags?' yelled a voice from ground control.

'I left them behind at the last minute,' he replied, a little shamefaced. 'I got a call on my mobile telling me that just an hour earlier there'd been an increase in the price of wine at the bar on the main square of my village, you know, the one just beside the ruins of the Roman chapel, and that distracted me a bit, I have to admit. But now, my friends, I'm ready to carry out my duty according to your instructions.'

And he'd hardly finished speaking when he came across a family of moon people who were studying him carefully.

'The Spaniard has arrived,' said the father to his son. 'Go back into the house and tell your mother to put on the satellite TV on so we can see what they're saying on Earth.'

And the boy obediently went away and his sister, as still as a statue, stayed there staring at the spasmodic jerking of the still-smoking machine, and at the man disguised as an old-fashioned beekeeper who was carrying out a precarious balancing act on the lunar floor.

'He arrived sixteen minutes later than the time you predicted,' she said to her father. And the astronaut took off his helmet, ran a hand through his hair, looked into the spaceship's camera and lifted up his jacket to reveal a t-shirt with the words 'I made it!' written in five different languages.

'How old are you?' he asked, looking at the girl. 'And where the hell are the kiosks and the table-football tables and the border posts of the free Moon.'

And then all the moon people stopped at once in the middle of their various activities – exercises in nocturnal contemplation, group harpsichord classes, pony-trekking amongst the craters, and supervision of the oxygen factories – and started telling each other that the Spaniard had arrived until they had spread the news all across the moon: 'It was written in our ancient science-fiction books that unpunctual men would one day arrive from the Earth to teach us the concept of quality of life.'

'The TV's broken!' the boy yelled from the door of his

house. 'Mum says she can't understand a thing because the picture's all fuzzy and instead of news from Earth the only thing she can get to come on is a kind of chat show where the guests all yell at each other and accuse one another of secret love affairs and marrying for money and ugly plastic surgery!'

'Some damned thing must be interfering with the televisual cultural programme of our spaceship!' the astronaut protested. 'It's funny because it's finally started working on the moon when it didn't work all the way here. But never mind, I'll fix it tomorrow, after breakfast.'

'Hey, what the hell do you think you're looking at?' asked a tall, blonde moon woman standing at the edge of her swimming pool.

'Oh, nothing,' he replied, 'nothing.'

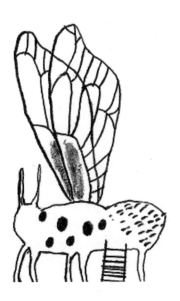

The Moon in the Wastepaper Bin

'So, it's midnight,' Cinderella said to herself, 'the underground stations are closed, the taxi drivers are on a two-day
hunger strike, and I have to run out of the party now, for
heaven's sake!'

And she curtsied to the prince, scribbled down her
email address for him on a page torn from her diary, and
ran quickly down the marble staircase, leaving behind
the giant *Pulp Fiction* poster and the stand selling Bloody
Marys with or without Tabasco sauce, and the exhibition of
broken helmets, and the 'No Entry' sign, and ran out into
the street without pausing for breath. And she had barely
left the building when she was approached by a man with
sunken eyes and a black goatee who took off his top hat to
greet her.

'Do you have any money you could lend me?' he asked,
persuasively. 'I'll pay back double what you give me, one of
my ancestors was a viceroy in the Indies and a champion
bridge player, and what's more I've got friends in high

places, I can get you an interview and make you famous, believe me, I can make you a star.'

Cinderella looked at him closely and saw a tape recorder hidden in the pocket of his coat and, as she didn't want any trouble, she called a policeman, who came over looking suspicious and looked her up and down.

'Well, young lady,' he said finally, 'you've got a haircut like a convict, you're wearing a gold safety pin through one ear, you smell funny and it seems to me like you must be mixed up in drugs.'

'No, no,' she said with alarm, 'I'm a student in the last year of high school and I just crashed the party in the palace because my boyfriend works there, in the plumbing department.'

'This is a responsible city, young lady,' said the policeman, 'and there's no reason why I should believe you; the slightest little thing could bring you under suspicion of belonging to the club of con-artists that you hear so much talk about these days, who have made lying common practice all over the country since the beginning of the media revolution and the crisis in the fairy kingdom.'

And just at that moment a team of cameramen and TV reporters appeared.

'We were waiting for you, Cinderella,' they shouted, 'we want to know if there's any truth in the rumours linking you to the prince, and if you ever go sunbathing on desert islands.'

'No, no, no!' answered Cinderella. 'I'm just a normal girl, I like Carlo Gesualdo, Jimi Hendrix and Thelonius Monk,

I live with my mother in a third floor flat with no balcony, I get top marks in botany and believe in world peace.'

The man in the top hat had made the most of the confusion and left, but not before stealing a microphone and tucking it into his coat pocket along with the tape recorder.

'I'll call you a cab,' said the policeman, facing the cameras with a look of great authority.

'They're on strike,' she said. 'They want police protection after midnight because the kingdom hasn't been the same since the arrival of those conmen with their plans to build theme parks and their promises of fame for all. They say that life has changed around here. They say that the city is under siege by an army of reporters from the tabloid press who camp outside it day and night, trying to blind it and drive it crazy with camera flashes and, in the name of freedom, they deny us the right to live without the whole world knowing our business. They urge us to give ourselves up to their attacks and let ourselves be invaded for the greater good.'

'Tell me about it, I was a taxi driver before I was a policeman, and I've seen it all,' he replied. And he lowered his voice to make sure that only Cinderella would be able to hear him.

'I've seen the kind of reporters you were talking about,' he whispered. 'I've seen them spread themselves out over the city like hungry crocodiles at nightfall, positioning themselves on top of the traffic lights, up the church towers, inside rubbish bins, behind the ministers' carriages, and under manhole covers. I've seen them examining the silence as if they suspected it, and following our trail and shouting: "Who knows anything about anybody's love life?" And I've heard their shouts disappear like wounded echoes through the deserted streets. I know the future, my girl, and I can't sleep at night.'

While the policeman was talking, the television crew carried on filming the scene, whispering, 'This surely marks the beginning of a major new debate about whether or not the prince should be able to marry just whoever he likes.'

'Well, when all's said and done, we are the people,' said one of the sound technicians.

'Yes,' they said, 'we are the people and we have the right to know the private lives of celebrities to see whether anything bad ever happens to them, because there's no better consolation for the masses than being able to rejoice in the misfortune of those they envy. Come on Cinderella, tell us about yourself, have you ever been abroad?'

'Yes,' Cinderella answered, 'once I went to Rome on a school trip, and I saw the gate which the barbarians poured in through.'

And after she'd said this she began to feel dizzy.

'Where's my pillow?' she asked. 'My head hurts and I'm beginning to worry that this might be a dream.'

'If it was, what the hell would that make us?' asked the policeman, looking more and more nervous. 'That's a pretty poor excuse at this time of night, and the only thing I'm sure about in this whole sorry mess is that you smell of cannabis.'

And Cinderella bit her lip. 'Damn,' she thought, 'that's the prince's smell.'

And she started to run and crossed the street through a red light, leaving behind the reporters who were shouting after her, 'What kind of underwear do you use, Cinderella? What do you think of the class struggle?' And then, when she'd got far enough away from them, she took off her shoes, which were beginning to pinch her feet, and threw them into a cast iron wastepaper bin. 'How beautiful the moon looks reflected in the iron,' she murmured.

And then Cinderella had a kind of revelation. The moon was a dancer who crossed over the city on tiptoes, and who had now climbed into the wastepaper bin to rest for a moment, shy and breathless, before continuing on the path she had always followed, since long before the kingdom was attacked by those hordes of liars, through centuries of invasions, pilgrimages, inventions, duels and heartbreaks which had painstakingly woven together the history of the world. And Cinderella also realised that the moon would continue its dance night after night, leaving behind all those who lived and dreamed and died under its light, the light of an artist with her makeup removed, of a muse painfully tired of the repetitive secrets of that rattling planet which she had no choice but to patrol in the dark.

It was almost dawn. Cinderella set out barefoot on the road towards home, taking a detour through the park to see the moon seek out a new hiding place amongst the leaves of the ash trees. And, when she was sure there was nobody else around, she stopped and took a deep breath, unbuttoned her leather jacket, and started to furtively touch her shoulders, chest and navel; and then she held her nose.

'That policeman was right,' she thought, 'I need a shower.'

Not Just Rock and Roll

The sun was beating down on Madrid as the people squeezed into the stands and onto the grass of the stadium. There were lots of beautiful girls there in the early evening light, like hunter goddesses who were invisible during the day, who it would be impossible to imagine as part of the hated routine of nine to five, who fearlessly handled the secret simplicities of a sublime, feline love, a love to redeem the anguish of the world, a love unattainable to all those unworthy of even touching the straps of their vest tops; who had brought together all of their dark, infuriating beauty simply because, behind the scenes, in their dressing room, five Englishmen were also feeling the heat and speaking together in low voices. There was no need for them to tune their numerous guitars; somebody had already done that for them.

And suddenly the sky split in two and emptied its furious load of storm and hail over Madrid.

'Now,' said Mick Jagger, 'let's go out now.'

With No Left Hand

'Look, Miguel,' said the editor, 'it's nothing personal. Believe me. Well, I know you believe me, or at least I believe you believe me. But I just can't publish it like this. Take out three hundred pages and then we'll talk. The stories are good, I'll give you that, but they interfere with the general rhythm of the plot, and they weigh the book down. And we're at the beginning of the twenty-first century here, for God's sake, look around you, look at the footballers and politicians selling their memoirs, look at the bestsellers lists. And then you come to me with a manuscript more than a thousand pages long describing the adventures of a Golden Age nobleman who goes nuts from too much reading. That tops it all, it really does. You make reading sound like a risk in these dark times when the people spend their evenings brain-dead in front of the telly, watching designer witches lecturing about weddings, affairs and divorces into microphones dipped in sulphuric acid. We editors have to compete with characters who would frighten the life out of a nightclub in Gomorrah just to sell a measly book, and you come to me with this. Oh yes, the style is good, that goes without saying; well controlled, not completely lacking in humour, and you really capture the tone of the period. But you're not Quevedo, or Lope, or Góngora, and you didn't live their lives however much you might wish you did. You are Miguel Cervantes Saavedra, a civil servant on leave from the tax office, you were born forty or so years ago in Alcalá, where as far as I know your father still works as a doctor for the National Health Service; and it just so happens that you lost your left hand in Turkey on your honeymoon, when a mad aspiring terrorist threw a grenade in the Grand Bazaar in Istanbul while you were haggling over some bangles for your wife. And I can hardly sell that story as a cosmopolitan rebellion, can I? Your CV is useless, you don't give a damn about political correctness, you don't speak a single regional language other than your own. If there happened to be an Alcalá dialect, or perhaps a different language for Castilla La Mancha to link you somehow to the struggle of minority cultures, then maybe we could do something for you, as long as you remembered to criticise the centralism of our long-suffering capital and to say something in favour of a federal state. But, in all seriousness, Miguel, you're just a dead weight.'

And Miguel looked at the trees outside the window, past the table, behind the head of the editor, who he knew to be an intelligent man, and who was talking to him now with the tone of someone who wouldn't object to making an exception and chatting about literature with a sense of humour and the sincerity of an expert, if only he had the time.

'I've been in prison,' he said tentatively.

'Yes,' the editor admitted, 'yes, that's good. But you don't have that bad guy look, quite the opposite in fact; it's as if you must have been there out of some misunderstanding, like they must have made some kind of a mistake. You act as if you expect the whole world to become more sophisticated just so they can understand you, just because your work deserves it; as if you think your pig-headed refusal to make any concessions is going to seem sexy to people who feel important when they're chattering away on their multimedia phones in shopping centre car parks, who get nervous waiting for a goal at football stadiums, who mistake pills for reducing cholesterol for residual fragments of the philosopher's stone. Yes, yes, I know you don't much like the way things are headed on this planet of ours; neither do I. As that Shakespeare you're so devoted to says in *Macbeth*, 'Fair is foul and foul is fair.' That's just the way things are; those old witches have seen their aesthetic pattern become a reality over the course of the centuries. And I hardly need to add that if Shakespeare himself suddenly appeared with his manuscripts under his arm at London's modern day publishing houses he'd receive a well-deserved slap on the wrist, like the one that I'm so generously handing out to you, and an invitation to stop flirting with dead muses and sign up as soon as possible to the great scam of literature. No, Miguel, I don't like the world much either. But at least I try to enjoy what's left of it while it lasts. When China becomes a global superpower we'll cover our heads in ash and go begging forgiveness at the American embassy, and look for hamburger dealers under manhole covers, and watch with Christian resignation as the high altar at the Almudena cathedral is turned into a stand selling spring rolls. Seriously, Miguel. Three hundred pages shorter. Oh, and it wouldn't be a bad idea if that shy little Dulcinea could get topless before page fifty. Do what I say, come back and see me and then we'll see whether we can squeeze anything out of the town councils of the villages you mention in the book. Hey, why are you looking at me like that? Do I look like some kind of a monster?'

And Miguel stood up, wrapped his scarf around his neck, put on his jacket, and smiled for the first time.

'No,' he said. 'No. You look like a windmill.'

The Trouble with Secrecy

And you've forgotten the night when your mother closed the door and told you in an excited voice that there's a conspiracy, you know, an ancient bond between parents which has been passed down throughout history to make children lose their innocence quickly so they can familiarise themselves as soon as possible with the disappointments of this world, but the truth is that the Three Wise Men *do* exist. And you ran out of the room and in the hallway you bumped into Melchior trying on a pair of ski-boots with a huge smile on his face.

'We don't have this sort of thing up there,' he told you. 'There's no snow, it was all stolen by the devils during that famous rebellion of theirs and they took it all away with them to decorate hell.'

You rushed down the stairs and once you got out to the street you saw Caspar on his camel, yawning as he waited for the traffic lights to change.

'What do you think of my velvet frock-coat?' he asked

you. 'I bought it, or should I say exchanged it, on Carnaby Street for a pair of Japanese radios. What do you think of that? I was just like Columbus on his travels, oh yes, I remember him as a little boy, we brought him a map which I designed myself, decorated with snakes and roaring waves and smoky-coloured whales. Isn't it funny how things turn out? If it wasn't for that little fancy of mine we wouldn't have to travel to America these days with all the trouble that comes along with it; Balthazar was arrested once in Mississippi and had to show them a false passport forged by God himself – ah, here he comes, unflappable as always!'

And on the corner of the street you saw Balthazar polishing his silver spurs with a handkerchief made of Turkish silk, and you asked him how things were going.

'Well, I was just speaking to your mother while you were asleep,' he replied, 'and reminiscing about the old days when you were a little baby and you still believed in your parents. One time she offered me a glass of water and I said that all I needed was a half an ounce of hash. "I don't take drugs," she said. "I do," I replied, "I need them fairly often, especially when I'm working and have to face up to this thankless secrecy which is so compromised by the timeless nature of divine decisions, but anyway, that's enough about me. Have a look in my rucksack.'

And you looked and you saw the complete works of the Marquis de Sade and a signed photo of Aretha Franklin, and some campaign binoculars made by Prussian soldiers in Jena, and a lemon-yellow foldable sun umbrella, and, right at the bottom, a little crimson-coloured satin bag with the words *Made in Afghanistan* sewn into it in gold thread. And he got onto his camel.

'I don't expect you to keep this secret,' he said with a sigh, 'but at least be selective about it, okay?'

Nobility and Botany

The girl closed the door of the lift behind her, and walked into the throne room with the pea in her hand.

'It's not a bad test actually,' she said. 'In my kingdom it's known as an old trick which was used for many generations before being declared obsolete. It's true that it kept me awake, but I'd like to make a few complaints.

'Since I couldn't sleep, I got up and looked out of the window and I saw a wounded deer wandering through the park with an arrow in its back, and it made me think about the need to kill animals, which I imagine must be widespread in this nation, perhaps also amongst poachers who are driven to it by hunger. I opened the drawer of the bedside table and I found a magazine with some garish photos of the Sporting Club in Monte Carlo and some of its regular patrons, which depressed me. I started rummaging through the CD racks and I couldn't find anything by Janis Joplin. I turned on the radio and tuned in to an international conference of defence ministers, and one in particular stood out because he was raving about the marvels of Ukrainian aeroplanes. I looked through the DVD collection and I came across a horrific selection of recent Oscar winners, including *Titanic*, for God's sake; I'd rather smash my head against an iceberg than call Leo DiCaprio an actor. It's strange seeing what's become the cultural norm these days; if Plato and Praxiteles lifted up their heads and saw what sort of thing was going on today, they'd rush out straight away to buy some hemlock from the nearest supermarket.

'Now I have to stop and take a deep breath because I get angry just thinking about what I've just said; but I'll continue. By now I was seething with irritation so I went out into the corridor and opened the balcony window to see what was going on in the town. A man with a cherry-coloured cape and breeches made of Belgian cloth was climbing down a thatched roof risking his neck to crawl in at a window where a woman was waiting for him with a cuckoo clock in her hand while below them, in the street, a blind beggar was saying that he'd fought for his king and country, and was handing a psaltery case around tables occupied by a gang of night-owls drinking beer out of tankards and talking at the top of their voices about Bentleys and Ferraris in that gloating way that people have when they're delighting in comparing their good fortune with the misery of the world. A little further on there was a lodging house and I saw a line of anorexic, bleary-eyed girls the same age as I am, queuing outside, looking for somewhere to stay in the city for a while so they could each have a chance with the prince; they were all carrying maps of Hollywood in their pockets and had broken lip liners hanging around their necks. I could tell one of them came from Hong Kong because she had kept the price tag and label on her Gucci bag to show that it wasn't a fake; another one came from Minsk, and had that half scornful and half soulless look of someone who feels she's already wasted too much of her life selling her beauty off far too cheaply; another was from Buenos Aires and was saying that everyone in her country had arrived in a boat; another one had a Sheffield accent and was talking about giving new life to the monarchy as an institution by bringing it up to date with the mixed, multicultural character of our times. And now I think it's about time that I got the point of this story.'

Before she continued talking, the girl looked around her. In the centre of the room, on the Persian carpet, was a shiny silver plate bearing half a dozen *amanita muscaria* mushrooms. A few steps away, a halberdier was standing to attention while a bluebottle buzzed determinedly around his face.

The young woman took a deep breath.

'I don't know what you must think of me,' she said, 'but the fact is that I got completely drenched in the storm last night and was just looking for a decent place to spend the night, and the intuition of my breeding did the rest. And now I'd like to say two things. The first is that it's ignoble by definition to lecture people about nobility, and so I won't say anything more about this old trick of yours with the pea; coarseness is so overwhelmingly widespread in this world that you only need to distance yourself from it a bit and you'll find friends who think as you do, not all that many of them but just enough to get by. And the second thing is that it's not marriage that I'm looking for. In fact, it makes me feel sick just thinking about spreading my legs in front of a group of royal gynaecologists, who I imagine would be old, nosey and just a little lecherous. The way I see things, that undignified ritual perversely has a lot in common with an exercise practised impulsively nine months earlier, just a simple moment of pleasure which, when I think about it properly, I could quite easily manage without. And it's just not fair. I don't see why I should have to pay such a high price just for one day coupling my body with that of someone who, in the best case scenario, would put on a little mask in the delivery room in a fine display of sympathy, and squeeze my hand, and go out and tell the press that he had an heir and then go straight off to call his nanny and his lover. No, no, that's just not what I want. But the pea really did keep me awake, that's the honest truth, and when I went back into my room I ended up lying on the floor because, well, I don't need to go into it now but I might as well tell you that I took a course in yoga last year, and I was just trying to settle down to sleep when I heard all the palace's ladies-in-waiting hurrying indiscreetly along the carpets on the floor below me, quickly swapping sets of keys and making such a racket that you'd have thought we were minutes away from the last Ash Wednesday in history. And now I'm so tired that I'm not even sure if I fell asleep in the end and that this isn't just part of my dream.'

The queen was glaring at her like a newly-sculpted gargoyle, but the girl didn't back away.

'Anyway,' she said, 'I've brought you back your talisman.'

And she looked around her again and saw that the halberdier was still standing unshaken at his post, and the bluebottle was now flying randomly around the room, looking a little lost.

And then she took ten determined steps forward, and left the pea on the steps to the throne. And then she felt her clothes, glad to see they were finally dry.

Time Out

They started arriving slowly, with cautious steps, as if unsure of themselves, as if worried that they might be struck down at any moment by a sudden feeling of reverence, and little by little they spread across the square until they had covered it completely.

Once they found themselves all squeezed in there together the mood changed and they started openly looking at one another with an almost rude curiosity. There were desert nomads proudly holding the reins of their camels and occasionally beating their drums out of fear of losing their companions in the crush of the crowd. There were Chinese torturers with painstakingly curled black hair who were fanning themselves with peacock-feather fans and struggling to breathe under the oppressive Mao collars on their nylon jackets, and astronomers from Cabo Verde waving maps of Saturn in the air, and anarchists from Minnesota studying books on phonetics, and deliverymen from Cuzco handing out free painkillers because today's a special day, they said, and we're all brothers. And of course there were Romans too: women with plucked eyebrows and men holding their heads up high as if posing for their picture on a coin.

And finally the pope took the advice of the canticles and stepped out onto the balcony.

'What do you want?' he asked them.

'We're here to protest against mortality!' they shouted back at him in an avalanche of different languages. A group of Eskimos waved a banner in Danish demanding immortality for those who work for it.

An Englishwoman turned to her husband and whispered, 'I have to say that the Archbishop of Canterbury, when you see him in person, looks far more majestic than the papists' infallible guru.'

'We have to respect the views of the majority, as we agreed,' said her husband diplomatically, without looking up from his copy of the *News of the World*.

Then a spokesman stepped forward to speak on behalf of the demonstrators and read a manifesto in Latin.

'After deep discussions,' he said, 'we have decided to put aside our differences of creed, which at this moment seem of secondary importance, and have agreed to come here, to the centre of world religion, to express our shared conviction that what we have to go through and suffer is simply not fair. No, your Holiness. It's not fair that we should be weighed down with uncertainty about our final destiny for all our lives, on top of all the other hardships which keep us in a permanent state of discomfort, as well as being blackmailed to do the right thing left, right and centre under the threat of eternal punishment. We have realised that we are all united by the same anxiety, and because of this we want your Holiness to communicate our protest to He who has appointed you as His representative on Earth. We will not move from here until we've had an answer to our request, which is the following: we want Him to declare a "time out" in the life of the earth, during which time not a single creature on this miserable planet will be struck down by death's crushing blow so that, when we've received this guarantee, we will all be able to feel safe at last, and breathe as freely as if we'd never read stories about original sin. In short, we want to vent our frustration, your Holiness, because where there's death, nobody can live.'

And the pope thought in silence for a few moments, and scratched his chin.

'Look, all of you,' he said, 'I'm an old man and I share your concerns, believe me, I understand them well, but I fear your demands are beyond my powers. I can ask Him for you, of course, and I might even be able to negotiate a little more excitement and less tedium in your view of the world's landscapes: you will have emerald-green skies, sand as blue as sapphires for your beaches, snow as red as leopard's blood for your mountains and water as transparent as Bohemian crystal for your rivers, which furthermore will run full of nymphs and sirens with an open, liberal attitude with whom, if it's any consolation, you will have the chance to live out your most primitive fantasies of entertainment. I might even be able to get you a reduction in the hole in the ozone layer; but oh, my friends, I can't get you the thing you ask for.'

'We won't move from here,' the spokesman repeated, and his phrase was echoed in a storm of defiant applause, and the first torches began to glimmer in the night amid shouted threats to set fire to Rome.

'But not the taxi stand in the Piazza del Popolo,' someone protested.

'Not the Trevi Fountain,' shouted someone else.

'Not the statue of Giordano Bruno,' somebody else begged from the crowd.

'What time is the Rome versus Lazio match?' asked a Spanish demonstrator holding a transistor radio to his ear.

And a sharp, sickle-shaped silence spread over the square and trembled in the air like an old-aged acrobat.

'It's already started,' answered an Italian, who understood the question. 'I'm from Milan and a big Inter fan, what team to do you support?'

And the Spaniard answered but nobody heard him because suddenly a tumult of voices arose declaring: 'I'm a Glasgow Rangers fan', 'I support Dynamo Kiev', 'I support Ethiopian Coffee from Addis Ababa', 'I'm with Yokohama Marinos', and 'I'm an Alianza de Panama fan.'

And then, above all this noise, they began to hear a dull roar which they hadn't noticed until now coming from the Olympic stadium with the swelling force of a sea stirred up by a stormy wind and, little by little, larger and larger groups of dejected demonstrators started leaving the square, speeding up the further away they got. And the

Swiss guards stopped frowning and pointing their halberds at people and let a group of South Koreans take their photographs in exchange for half a dozen CDs of music for Zen meditation.

And the pope improvised a good-natured, routine blessing with the confidence of someone who knows their job inside out, and then turned away from the dispersing crowd and glanced surreptitiously at his secretary.

'Please,' he whispered to him, 'can you find out the score?'

Conditional Eternity

'And so you want to take a look outside', said God; and he opened the heavy, creaking door to let her out. She felt a little uncomfortable in the long satin dress with the vine leaf pattern that she had put on for the occasion, and she followed him with uncertain steps, a little downcast, as if worried that she wouldn't know how to behave.

'Hello Dante', said God. 'That's Dante, the one with the pointed nose and the red tunic, he's an impressive poet although a little bit of a fantasist, if I'm honest with you; he's a member of the White Guelph party and he misses his lover because, and this is something you need to know, outside of Paradise the men pine after women in a most peculiar way, first lifting them up to the altars of suffering, and then reducing them to the rubble of literature. And those over there are Vopos from Berlin who miss their old guard duties and march up and down the streets in their studded boots to stop anybody sneaking in here because they know that this is just for you and Adam – which reminds me, where is Adam?'

And she blushed.

'He wasn't interested,' she said. 'He stayed at home watching videos.'

'Ah, look,' He said, 'that green patch over there is Africa, a huge place full of machetes and drums and dead elephants, which always makes me feel sad to look at because it brings to mind that ancient contrast, so infuriating and so human, between the promise of the future and the misery of the present. That fat man over there with the wig, the one sitting on the floor with the tankard of Lowenbrau next to the statue of a Baroque angel is Bach – Hi Bach, how's it going? Bach composes loads of religious music, which for the most part I like, although sometimes it embarrasses me a bit, frankly. I never intended to be sung to with such pomp and show; for me the important thing was always just a question of making a quiet effort on a daily basis, you know, and not about isolated, more or less over-elaborate rituals which actually distract from the continuous practice of virtue; but anyway, that's just the way things have turned out. And over there is the Utah desert; it's full of Mormons who insist they know me very well, as do a lot of people as it happens, and again I find it best to opt for a discreet silence. And over there you can see the pollution over Mexico City, right at the back, next to the volcano. I seem to remember that I like that city, but I can hardly see it very clearly these days –'

'I'm feeling a bit tired,' said Eve. 'This is all too much for just one visit.'

'I did warn you,' He said, 'but you insisted, and look! There's a Greenpeace zodiac, nice kids, I'll tell you another day about their campaign, they spend their whole lives getting squirted with water from the hosepipes of one important ship or another and – ah, before I forget, that over there is Beverly Hills, a very expensive place full of charlatans dressed in dinner jackets who criticise the government while they drug themselves up to the eyeballs in garish Cadillacs, and I shouldn't really be telling you this but they need to change their tastes as soon as possible, or they'll be in big trouble.'

'Please, I want to go home,' said Eve. 'I want to see whether the fruit trees in my garden are flowering yet.'

'So, you feel differently about things this morning then?' asked God.

'Yes, I do,' she admitted in a studiously humble voice. 'But then, I suppose I'm allowed to make mistakes, aren't I?'

'Yes,' he replied, 'yes, you are. For now.'

Today

'We have a very special guest tonight,' said the TV presenter. And she looked at the audience, but they did not meet her gaze. They were all too busy looking for themselves in the monitor hanging from the studio ceiling to see if they were on screen, and nudging each other excitedly when they saw that, yes in fact the camera was pointing right at them.

'Our guest,' said the presenter, 'is one of many people who has something to say and who deserves our attention because of the profoundly human content of the message that they can give us. One of those many people who can reveal to us the cruel nature of today's society. We won't reveal his name or show his face which, as you can see, is covered by a mask. The reason for this is that he is understandably scarred by his experience, as you all will also be when you hear his story. But I can give you a taster and tell you right now that this man at my side, this brave man who has just signed a contract with one of this country's major publishing houses to get his testimony down in writing, saw his life irreversibly changed one day when, while taking a walk through the distant southern lands where he lives, he was suddenly assaulted and sodomized by a penguin.'

The presenter paused for a few seconds, hoping that she had made an impact on the audience, and she suddenly noticed that two women in the back row had dropped down dead on the floor with smoke coming from their heads, as if they had been struck by lightning. This was followed by a confusion of broken cables and blown fuses which the technicians rushed to fix while more and more people of both sexes were keeling over in their seats, as dead as the first two women. One camera continued functioning and was filming the whole scene, and the presenter put one hand to her earpiece, listened to some instructions, frowned, and then began to react promptly to the news.

'Can I have your attention, please,' she said. 'Ladies and gentlemen, we have just received information indicating that the end of the world has begun, and that destruction on a huge scale is unfolding in numerous places across the planet, including in this studio. It appears that various cities have already been devoured by flames, and that the death count is rising quickly everywhere. Right now our monitor is displaying images of the Kremlin in Moscow, almost entirely consumed by fire, and we can see the Russian president calling a taxi because the chauffeur of his official car has made an escape amid widespread panic, which is also taking place, it's terrible to see, on the Great Wall of China, now crammed with citizens of that country who, you can see as well as I can, are trying in vain to take refuge amongst the stones of their most emblematic building which, and this is truly incredible, is now crumbling to the ground. The Great Wall of China, my dear friends, has ceased to exist in the space of just a few seconds. Heartbreaking. These images, I remind you again, are coming to us right now, live on screen. And this is the Casa Rosada in Buenos Aires, which also appears to be engulfed in flames, we can see the country's president rushing out to look for a cash machine. But now the image is blurring, this new picture is, let me see, this is a jail in the state of Alabama, where a group of Afro-American prisoners are trying to break their chains with hammers while the guards are galloping away at high speed down the motorway.'

'To recap, ladies and gentlemen, for those of you have just tuned in, the end of the world has begun and in fact here, in our own studios, we can confirm that our audience is being wiped out by lightning bolts and that there are only a few survivors now left in the stands, but this is a television station and we have a duty to our viewers, and we have to get our priorities straight. New images are continuing to arrive live from a desert, yes, we can confirm that it is the Sahara, which as you can see is covered in ice – how strange! – and a jeep has got trapped containing half a dozen presidents-for-life who, according to our sources, have abandoned their respective countries and are trying to escape to wherever they can, carrying a suitcase full of rhinoceros horns. And the image we're seeing now appears to be from Gibraltar; we can see a monkey with its tail on fire climbing up a drug trafficker's yacht, and, yes, we can confirm it now, the end of the world has officially arrived. These events have caught us by surprise, because you never imagine that the end of the world is going to happen today. But it has in fact happened, and we're live on air, and I'm sure that the people watching at home would like to hear more details about what our guest has to tell us. My dear friends, listen carefully to find out what that penguin did. Don't go away.'